CHAPTER ONE

Alice walked along the crowded deck with absolutely no eyes on her whatsoever. *Le Mistral* was Paris' most luxurious event boat and she had hoped that she would be able to attend the evening's party in a dazzling frock but, as always, she was in the smart but distinctly anonymous uniform of a waiter. None of the guests at the glittering party would suspect that she was here to do anything other than serve canapés and refill champagne glasses. She passed a woman wearing a maroon velvet gown and offered her one of the bite-size treats from the silver tray on her palm. The woman's companion smiled at the air just above Alice's head and took four.

Beyond them, at the bow of the boat, Alice could see Claude, the older spy she was on the mission with, elegantly kitted out in a perfectly cut evening jacket accented with jet. With his dark hair slicked back into a perfect quiff, and his chiselled features that always drew admiring glances, Claude had, as usual, gathered a crowd of women, each trying to catch his attention. One of them touched him lightly on the elbow and whispered an amusing remark. Her laughter at her own joke floated across the night air to where Alice stood, wondering if she would draw attention to herself if she disappeared to the galley kitchen for a rest. She had been on her feet and forcing a polite smile for two hours.

Claude was rising. Waving an empty champagne glass at his companions, he strode across the deck towards a waiter carrying a tray packed with sparkling glasses. As he passed Alice, Claude tapped his glass lightly and rhythmically with the side of his diamond signet ring and Alice's eyes widened at the sound. Three short taps and two longer ones. Three in Morse code. It meant three o'clock and it was a signal to Alice to look to her right. Alice flicked her eyes in that direction and spotted her prey.

The man looked ordinary enough, but then they always did. He was watching the patch of deck where a scattering of couples had set up an impromptu dance floor, laughing and falling into one another as *Le Mistral* moved up and down on the sway of the river Seine.

They were nearing a bridge and Alice could see couples leaning over the parapet, watching the boats pass beneath them, the golden sunset reflecting off the water into their faces. Alice saw the man glance upwards. She followed his gaze up to the middle of the bridge. Between a couple caught in a kiss and a man lifting his small child to wave at the party boats was a woman in a severe grey coat and hat. Her eyes locked with those of the man and Alice saw her nod once.

I was right, she thought. The man was on this boat to pass information and that had been the signal that it was safe to do so.

Alice felt the man brush past her. He was on the move.

Ignoring the hand of one partygoer who had just spied the salmon mousse pastries on her tray, Alice set off after him at a discreet distance, trying to look like she just *happened* to be making her way towards the front of the boat. The man ducked inside to the main party room and Alice followed. The music was louder in here, the band in full swing, and the room was so crowded that Alice found it difficult to follow her quarry. She fixed her eyes firmly on the loose collar stud at the back of his neck and pushed her way through the room, weaving her way round a couple who had broken into a dramatic tango. The man had crossed the room and was about to exit to the opposite side of the boat. Alice was stepping

4

past a group at the edge of the room when she felt a tug on her elbow.

"Here, let me try one of these," said a girl in a pink evening dress, pursing her lips as she glanced over the pastries on Alice's tray. Alice smiled at her through gritted teeth, trying to keep her eyes on the man as he disappeared through the door and on to the deck.

"They all look so nice," the girl said, pouting. She put a finger to her lips and looked at her companion through thickly mascaraed lashes. "Why don't you choose, Silvie?"

The man had turned left, towards the front of the boat. Alice felt her foot tapping impatiently, but there was no way she could just hand over the entire plate and run. She glanced at the girl, her mind racing. The girl was wearing a chiffon gown in strawberry pink and her shoes were delicate pumps, not the sky-high heels of some of the other women. Alice breathed in and was hit by a scent of almonds in the girl's perfume. Alice smiled and selected a tiny treat from the middle of the tray – a froth of red on a biscuit base.

"I think this would suit Mam'selle," she said. "It is

strawberry almond mousse."

A delighted smile broke across the girl's face.

"Oh, how clever of you," she gushed. She popped the treat into her mouth, grabbed her companion's elbow and dragged her off to dance.

Alice turned on her heel and dashed out on to the deck.

The man was nearing the front of the boat now, where two women stood chatting, away from the noise and bustle of the party. Alice fixed her eyes on the man, watching to see if anything passed between them. Ahead she saw the lights of another party boat heading towards them, its music growing louder as it passed underneath a bridge. Alice glanced up. Like the others, this bridge was packed with couples. It would be so easy for someone to drop something down on to the deck. She had to make sure that she wasn't distracted.

She had nearly reached the small group when she heard the noise of clattering feet behind her and, with a high-pitched squeal, the girl in strawberry chiffon dashed past her. "Silvie, we'll be passing near the Eiffel Tower soon!" she squealed. "Oh, do come and see how beautiful it is. I think I just saw a shooting star!"

"In the middle of the city? Don't be foolish, Veronique," Silvie muttered.

Just ignore them, thought Alice, focusing on the man. The girl called Veronique grabbed the top rail on the boat's edge and stepped up on to a lower bar, leaning over the side.

The man had paused by the two women, his hand in his pocket. One of the women met his eye and she blinked, with the tiniest nod of her head. Alice edged forwards. The woman took a silver cigarette case from her pocket, clicked it open and offered a cigarette to the man. Alice could see a card tucked inside the case. She *had* to see what was written on it. She moved closer.

The other boat was upon them. The river swelled as it drew past and *Le Mistral* gave a lurch. Alice threw out a hand to steady herself as it pitched sideways, but too late to stop her tray slipping from her hand, the tiny cakes rolling across the deck. Behind her, Veronique gave a sharp scream. Ahead of her, the woman with the cigarette case slipped on the wooden decking and the card flew out and lodged itself in one of the ropes slung along the side of the boat. It was almost too good an opportunity.

Alice sprang forward, ready to pretend she wanted to return it to the woman, while carefully checking what was written on it. Her fingers had almost closed around the corner of the card when, out of the corner of her eye, she caught a flash of pink flying up, over the boat's rail. She whipped her head round, but she already knew that the girl was in trouble. The force of the lurching boat had thrown her over the side. All thoughts of the card disappeared as Alice flung out an arm and caught at Veronique's waist, hauling her back into the boat. The two of them fell to the floor, the girl crying in shock and fright.

As the girl's companion rushed to help her, Alice saw the man begin to slip away, making the most of the distraction. As the man passed the card he swiped it up and slipped it into his pocket. In a matter of seconds, he would be out of Alice's sight and the mission would have failed. She had to act quickly. She pushed Veronique into the arms of her companion Silvie and hauled herself to her feet. As she did so, she let her hand close on a tiny iced cake that had fallen from her tray, then she placed herself firmly in the man's way.

"Oh, Monsieur, what a shock," she cried, trying to look as distressed as possible. "This lady almost fell overboard and—"

"Yes, you should get her some water. She's clearly had a fright," he said, trying to step round Alice.

"A terrible, terrible fright," Alice echoed, stepping back in front of him. "Oh…" She put her hand to her forehead and pretended to slump into a faint. The man muttered something under his breath and hurried her to a chair.

"Stay there," he growled. "I'll fetch a steward."

Alice waited till he had left before she uncurled her fist. Laying in the centre of her palm was the white card. A quick dip into his pocket as she "fell" and it had stuck fast to the icing. She was about to slip it into her pocket when she saw Claude making his way along the deck. The older spy went to stand beside her and pretended to look out over the water.

"Did you get it?" he asked in a low voice. Alice nodded and slid the card along the railing towards him. She watched his face carefully. She had not worked with Claude before and he was difficult to impress. Alice knew he was used to being paired with more senior spies on missions, so when directions had arrived the previous week announcing that he and Alice would be working together he had not bothered to hide his disappointment. But surely he would have to be impressed now. Alice had clutched victory from potential disaster. They had the card.

"What is this supposed to be?" growled Claude.

"What? It's the paper that was being passed to him. It was hidden in a cigarette case."

"Well, that can't be it," hissed Claude. "We were told they would be passing vital information, not a tatty slip of paper."

"Nothing was passed," insisted Alice.

"Weren't you watching the bridges? Think!"

Alice's blood ran cold. What if, in the moment when she glanced at the girl in the pink dress, something had been dropped from the bridge? What was it the girl had said? She thought she saw a shooting star. But it was only twilight – not dark enough to see shooting stars. Something else must have shot past, glinting in the evening sun.

"Someone dropped something metallic. Just before the man met the two women, something fell from the sky," Alice said, snatching back the slip of card and jamming it into her pocket.

"A film canister," nodded Claude. "Let's go."

They ran through the boat, almost colliding with partygoers. The boat was pulling into dock at a jetty on the side of the river and people were preparing, reluctantly, to go onshore. Claude pushed aside a waiter carrying a champagne bucket and Alice almost slipped as the ice sloshed across the floor.

"There!" cried Alice. The man was waiting by the gangway, chatting to the crew as they prepared to swing it out on to the bank. Claude careered down the deck towards him and the two of them locked eyes. For a second it looked like the man would turn and run, but instead he launched himself over the side of the boat, swung himself out and, with an expert somersault, landed safely on the riverbank.

Claude and Alice dashed to the edge of the boat and watched in dismay as the man turned and made his way towards a waiting taxi. Behind them, the crew began to roll the gangway out to the bank.

"Come on," muttered Claude. He leapt on to the end of the gangway, ignoring the cries of the crew, and began to run down it. Alice followed, but with nothing to anchor it at each end, the gangway began to sway alarmingly. Claude stumbled forwards, grabbing at the rails, Alice tripped and fell sideways towards the river. As she hit the edge of the gangway it lurched, toppling both of them into the river, to peals of laughter from the party guests. Alice spluttered her way toward the bank and hauled herself out. As she peeled river weeds from her hair she saw the man smirking at them and slipping into the back seat of his cab.

"It was a disaster," she said as they walked back along the river. "I fluffed it. What a waste of an evening." She jammed her hands deep into the pockets of her coat and kicked a loose stone into the river. They had spent hours planning this mission, and because Alice had allowed herself to be distracted by that foolish girl, it had almost been ruined.

Alice became aware of Claude watching her closely and she looked away across the river. She didn't need to meet Claude's eye to know that he was utterly disappointed and it was all Alice's fault. Alice hated getting things wrong in front of the older agents. She thought back to her first mission, on board France's luxurious Sapphire Express. That had so nearly turned to utter tragedy because of the mistakes she had made. Alice felt her cheeks colour up at the thought of it, even though it had been a huge success. She had been welcomed into the network of spies working for France against her enemies, but even so she still felt like she was always running to catch up. After her adventure on the Sapphire Express she had been determined to track down her Uncle Robert, but time had passed by with no word of him and she had been assigned to other missions. Then there were the other spies, who were all so much more glamorous and grown-up than her. She wished that her friend from the train, Penelope, was here to talk to, but Penelope was busy at finishing school in Nice and her letters were full of chat about lessons and parties, a far cry from her days of trying to uncover jewel thieves with Alice.

"It's annoying," said Claude. "But I overreacted; it was hardly your fault. You must have been distracted by that girl's accident."

"I shouldn't have let myself though," she said. "We failed and it was all my fault, letting that girl get in the way."

"Falling overboard is not getting in the way," Claude said sternly.

Alice shrugged.

"Alice Éclair, look at me!"

Alice was so surprised to hear Claude use her full name that she almost walked into a lamppost.

"Saving lives is never a disaster," Claude continued, his eyes boring into Alice's. "It's the job. If someone gets in the way because they need us, then we save them. If they distract us because they need us, then we save them. If saving them means we lose a codeword or a lead or even a set of plans, we still save them. Don't *ever* let me hear you be so careless about a human life again."

"But the mission…"

"So we didn't get the microfilm, Alice. It's only one piece of the puzzle. We'll find others. And if you had let that girl drown to save a slip of film… Well, I would be very disappointed in you."

CHAPTER TWO

Alice sat by Claude's kitchen fire, gently steaming as her clothes dried off, her hair swathed in a fluffy towel. There was no way she could go home to the pâtisserie she shared with her mother in the state that she had been in when they clawed their way out of the river. She had told her mother that she was going to see an art show at the Louvre, so weeds and wet clothing would be very difficult to explain. She had pulled everything from her pockets and the white card now lay discarded on the side of her chair.

Claude was brewing hot coffee on the stove, the smell filling the small room with caramel and chocolate tones. Alice inhaled deeply and her stomach rumbled. Though she had managed to sneak a few of the canapés at the party, she was very aware that they had missed dinner to get on to the boat.

As if reading her mind, Claude reached up to one of the shelves above the cooker and brought down an enormous cake tin.

"Here," he said, tossing it to Alice after unsuccessfully wrestling with the lid. "I kept some of that delicious orange cake you brought with you when we met. It's a few days old now, of course, but it should still be edible. Find a knife and we'll finish it off."

Alice grinned. "Edible" indeed! She was confident that it was going to be delicious. She had the lid off in a trice and cut them each a slab of the cake, chocolate sponge filled with an orange-infused ganache. It was a recipe that Alice was particularly proud of. The orange oil was *just* tart enough to cut through the sweetness of the chocolate. Alice sighed. She had baked it especially to impress Claude and get into his good books, and tonight she had undone all of that.

Alice licked the orange cream off her fingers and picked the card up. Although Claude had dismissed it as nothing, something about the way that the man had reached for it made her think that it must mean *something*. She frowned at the lettering. It was written in a strange, tilting script that made the letters look like they were not even English. Alice ran through every lettering system she knew, from Greek to Cyrillic, but she could not make out the letters of the code in any of them. Maybe Claude was right, it was just a meaningless card; the trademark of the cigarette maker, perhaps?

But then why would the man have picked it up? No. It meant something. Alice didn't always trust her ability, but she did trust her gut.

She tutted.

Claude dropped himself into the chair opposite Alice, leaned across the table and took the card from her. He twirled it in the tips of his fingers.

"Disgusting things, aren't they?" he said. "Cigarettes, I mean. I never understand why people smoke them. Are you still convinced this card means something?"

Alice nodded. "I know you think it's silly, it's just…"

"Your gut."

Alice nodded.

"All that work this evening just to get hold of this tiny thing," mused Claude.

Alice grimaced. Then a thought struck her.

"No, it wasn't," she said.

"Wasn't what?"

"No one was intended to get hold of it," she said, chasing after the thought that had just flickered across her mind. "The woman who had this in her cigarette case – she didn't give it to the man, she

18

showed it to him. He only picked it up because the wind whipped it out of the case and he had to."

"I don't see how that makes any difference," said Claude.

"Don't you see though?" Alice demanded. "It means that I'm looking at this all wrong. What if the card *being in the cigarette case* was the key to understanding it?"

She grabbed her bag from under the table and began rooting in the pockets. Thank goodness she had left it at Claude's before they set out for the boat. Out came train timetables, notebook after notebook, and her precious locked codebook that she had bought as a treat. It was embossed with a silver lightning flash, as Alice had adopted the codename *L'Éclair – the lightning bolt* – and she guarded it very carefully. It was not the book that she was looking for, however. She turned the bag upside down and gave it a good shake. Pencils and tins of peppermint rolled across the table, and tram tickets fluttered down into the sugar bowl.

"Alice, what *are* you doing?" asked Claude, but Alice ignored him. She whisked aside a handkerchief embroidered by her mother and snatched up the folded mirror that lay underneath it.

"What if it was in that case for a reason?" she said, holding out her hand. Claude passed her the card and, her heart beating wildly, Alice opened the mirror and laid the card inside, thinking, *Please let this work.*

"Daedalus!" she read.

Claude pushed himself away from his side of the table and dashed round to Alice. The card lay on the bottom of the mirror case and reflected above it, the lettering clear on the glass, was the word *Daedalus*, in a twisted script that only settled into letters when read as a reflection.

"He was never meant to take the card," Alice said. "That's why it was in the case. He was meant to read it reflected in the silver lid."

Alice stared at the code reflected in the mirrored glass. She had come so far in under a year, from being led by her uncle, the old master spy Robert Éclair, to working as an equal with France's other spies. If she had not uncovered Uncle Robert's secret and sent him into hiding, she might still be the naive girl he thought her to be.

"So you were right," Claude murmured. "Good

work, Alice. This confirms something we already suspected."

"What?" Alice asked.

"Wait there," said Claude. He stood and left the room. When he returned, he dropped a letter on to the table and smoothed it out. "Look here," he said, stabbing at one of the paragraphs. Alice leaned forwards. Claude had written it out in one of his more convoluted ciphers, but Alice recognised it at once and read it quickly and easily.

"The Daedalus plane will be able to fly further on one fuelling than any plane ever before. It could revolutionise warfare, keeping planes up in the air for longer..." she read aloud.

"You see?" Claude said. "It's a new plane, in development by the government. The plans are a closely guarded secret. So secret, in fact, that it took some considerable charm to convince my military contacts to even confirm that it exists. The Daedalus plane is a step forward in how far we can fly. Can you imagine if that technology was to be leaked? Enemy agents would be able to stay in the air for longer, silently gliding, taking photos of our military installations, plans of our towns, all sorts of information, and taking it straight back to the enemy. Or even dropping bombs on us and fighting for longer with our planes. The plans for this plane must not fall into enemy hands, and if this note means that someone is planning on sharing them..."

"But surely we have a list of who is working on them," Alice objected. "Isn't that where we should be starting?"

Claude cut her off. "We suspect a break-in," he said. "There are signs that the offices where the plans were kept were compromised. Someone may have copied the plans on to microfilm, and if that is so, then it's possible that is what was passed this evening."

"And I missed it," groaned Alice.

Claude shook his head. "No, Alice. I missed it. I dismissed this card as nothing, but really it gives us more evidence that the Daedalus plans are in danger. You see, we intercepted another message with 'Daedalus' in it last month, and that communication is very worrying indeed. It indicates that something is being planned for the World Fair next month. We don't know what, but it could be dangerous and it's linked somehow to Daedalus."

Alice's eyes widened at the mention of the World Fair. It was coming to Paris for the first time in years. Alice had been just a young child the last time the city played host to the spectacle, but so many of the customers of her mother's pâtisserie had told her stories about it. The whole world would flock to Paris, bringing examples of the best inventions, art and fashion that they had to display. Every country would have its own pavilion, each of which was being especially built near the Eiffel Tower, and across the river there would be pavilions dedicated to every industry and craft Alice could think of – from ceramics and sparkling jewellery to farming and every new innovation possible. The centre of Paris had been a building site for weeks now and one of Alice's favourite things to do on a rare day off from helping her mother in their boutique pâtisserie, *Vive Comme L'Éclair*, was to ride the funicular railway to Montmartre and gaze out over the city, watching the grand new buildings rise out of the dust and the industry and bustle far below.

"You can drop the daydreaming, Alice," Claude

said, breaking into Alice's thoughts. "It will be a prime opportunity for any spies. Paris will be full of political visitors from all over the world. It will be very easy for operatives to slip through undetected and connect with those who have access to our dearest secrets." He sighed. "We expect many traitors to make contact with the enemy during the course of the fair. We need to be there every day, but we need a way to look inconspicuous. And for some strange reason, this is where you and those skills everyone tells me about will come in very handy. Your little icing hobby is about to save the day."

He took a huge bite out of the chocolate cake and lost his train of thought for a second. Alice grinned. She had bristled at Claude calling her skills a "hobby", so she hoped he ate his words along with the rather excellent cake. Claude was not yet quite used to just how good a baker she was.

Claude recovered himself and had the good grace to look embarrassed. "Every spy in the world will be heading for Paris next month," he continued. "And you are going to be ready for them, in the most unlikely of places."

He slid a card across the table. Its lettering was

embossed and foiled in gold. Alice picked it up.

"The city is honoured to invite *Vive Comme L'Éclair* to exhibit their artistry and skill at –" Alice gasped. An invitation to represent France in the Tastes of the World pavilion was a great honour. Every pâtisserie, sweetshop and chef in Paris had been desperate to secure one, and now a place had fallen into her lap. Instantly, her head began to fill with ideas for cake designs. There was her famous Eiffel Tower Gateau to recreate, and maybe she could finally try the design she had been dreaming of since visiting the glorious palace at Versailles – a fountain crafted from fondant icing, topped with cascades of sugar so perfectly glazed they were transparent.

"I could fill it with rosewater and glycerine and make tiny fish that would look like they were moving…" she murmured, lost in thought. A cough from Claude brought her back to reality. She was there to be a spy. A place at the most sought-after exhibition in France was in her hands. How on earth was she going to impress the crowds *and* carry out a vital spying mission? She sighed. Somehow, she would just have to *make* it work.

CHAPTER THREE

Three weeks later, Alice shook out her apron and looked across the Tastes of the World pavilion. It was her third day at the fair and she felt as though an entire world of food had come to Paris. It was wonderful. Every stall was bustling with life and the air in the cavernous space was thick with scents that made Alice feel hungry in spite of her large breakfast. At a stall across the way, a woman from Russia was brewing up sweet teas in a magnificent kettle that Alice had, on the first day of the fair, discovered was called a samovar. The woman was busy crushing peppercorns with a mortar and pestle and mixing fragrant spices together in front of an entranced crowd. Beside her was a stall from Italy where a man threw dough high into the air, spinning it between his fingers and singing loudly to himself as flour billowed out with every clap of his palms. On the other side, a woman sat on the ground, turning tiny parcels wrapped with lemongrass in an open fire, counting out each one in a language Alice did not recognise. Alice wanted to breathe it all in, but there was work to be done, and *Vive Comme L'Éclair* would have nothing to offer the World Fair if she did not look lively.

As predicted, Madame Éclair had jumped at the chance to take part in the fair. "Just imagine," she had said, poring over designs for cakes and sweetmeats, "a chance to showcase what we can do at the greatest event Paris will see this century." She had sent Alice out with her sketchbook and told her not to come back till she had at least four new ideas for pastries and a design for an elaborate *croquembouche*. And now, here they were, in the centre of the World Fair, surrounded by stalls from all over the globe.

Unlike the stalls around them, Madame Éclair had decided not to cook at the fair. "Such hot work, Alice," she had said. "It would be far better for us to bake everything the night before and ice it at the fair. We can show off your artistry at its best then." So Alice busied herself ladling glistening white icing into a folded triangle of greaseproof paper topped with a silver nozzle. In front of her stood a replica of the fair crafted from melt-in-the-mouth squares of lemon biscuit. Alice had visited the fair the week before and sketched out the plan of every pavilion to make sure that she could recreate it perfectly, with each in its proper place. The glass roof of the jewellery pavilion was made from thin sheets of shimmering melted sugar. The ornate balustrades of the Ceramics pavilion were etched out in glossy icing. Even the blossom trees that lined the route to the ornamental glasshouses were represented, made from shaped icing and tiny pink blossoms. Like all of Alice's creations, it had garnered gasps from passers-by, but it was not merely there to show off her pâtisserie skills. It was a map, and if Alice was to hunt down spies, it might come in very useful indeed.

Alice was so engrossed in her work, adding extra dots of icing to the roof of one of the glasshouses, that she almost forgot where she was. When a lacquered fingernail suddenly tapped on the marbled top of the stall, Alice jumped with surprise and the piping bag split in her hand. She looked up and saw a young woman dressed in a smart two piece of bright-pink tweed. Her dark hair was swept into a neat chignon and she wore no make-up except for a gloss that highlighted the perfect shape of her mouth. She was also, without doubt, the most beautiful woman that Alice had ever met.

"Sorry, love," the young woman said. "I didn't mean to startle you. I'm meant to be at the Fashion pavilion, but this map has me all confused."

Alice put down her piping bag and snatched up a cloth to wipe the icing off her fingers. She leaned across the counter and took the map, which hung unfolded and was slightly torn, from the woman's hand.

"Well, we're here," she said, turning it so that the grand entrance of the Tastes of the World pavilion matched up with its tiny version on the map. "So I suppose you have to go through this hall, across the courtyard, turn to your left and ... yes, there you are." She stabbed at the space on the map marked *Fashion Today and Tomorrow*. "Are you going to one of the shows?"

The girl grimaced and took the map back. "No, worse luck. I'm *in* one. I'm one of the models for Monsieur Fouray's couture fashion show. One whole week of wearing dresses that are always too tight while having to smile, smile, smile. And I have to mind my manners. The other models come from quite posh backgrounds so I stick out like a whelk on an oyster dish. I'm lucky to get the job though.

The girl they originally picked twisted her ankle, so the agency called me."

Alice wasn't sure that she could think of anything that would be more fun. Dressing up in beautiful clothes and jewels and swanning around while everyone admired you sounded like a wonderful job.

"Anyway, thanks for the directions," the girl continued. "I'll try to get you a free ticket for one of the shows if you like. They're a bit dreary, but the clothes are gorgeous. I'll come back tomorrow with it if I can. Thanks again."

She folded the map up into her clutch bag and, with a wave of her hand, turned and dashed across the floor towards the exit, almost colliding with a man carrying a tray piled high with steaming noodle bowls.

Alice stared after her. For a minute she imagined herself sashaying down a stage in an organza ballgown, a glittering starburst necklace at her throat and her glossy chestnut bob swept to the side in an emerald clip. She sighed. It was no good wishing. She wiped the icing sugar off her hands and got back to work.

By three o'clock, hundreds of people had passed through the pavilion and Alice had been so busy demonstrating her icing techniques and talking to visitors about all the wonderful flavours that France had to offer that she had barely had time to think about the real reason she was here. Claude had arranged this spot in the middle of the food hall for a specific reason – sooner or later everyone who entered the hall would pass by. But the hall was so packed that Alice wondered how Claude, who she hadn't even *seen* since the fair began, expected her to do any spying. Besides, Madame Éclair kept her constantly busy. "This is such a good opportunity for us," she would repeat on an almost hourly basis, so Alice felt guilty for trying to sneak away. There was guilt, too, at knowing how much she was lying to her mother, but if she knew the truth about Alice's involvement in spying, she would be bound to put a stop to it at once. Alice could not risk that. The World Fair would be finishing in less than a week and she had a traitor to catch.

On the first day, she had been sure that she had seen a man lingering a little too long by the Indian

Spices stall, but it turned out that he was just waiting for his wife, who had left her parasol somewhere in Greece; and the woman who passed a folded paper to another by the Italian pastries on day two and who Alice followed around the hall for at least an hour turned out to be returning a dropped banknote. Only one really strange thing had happened since the fair opened – the button. On the second day, a man had stopped to admire Alice's biscuit model and a button from his coat had dropped into the middle of the almond-sugar gardens. Alice had reached to pick it out for him and dust it down, but he had swept her hand aside with a great cry of alarm (knocking over both the Italian pavilion and the Ceramics pavilion in the process) and had grabbed at it himself and hurried away. Such a fuss over a button. There was something odd about it all. Alice had tried to follow him, but Madame Éclair had gathered a group of passers-by around to watch an icing demonstration and Alice had, reluctantly, had to watch him hurry away.

Today, though, there was nothing, and Alice was feeling quite out of things when Claude wove his way through the crowd and passed by the stall with a burnt-orange silk square in his jacket pocket. Alice put down her icing bag. They had worked this code out in advance. Pink would mean "nothing to discuss". Blue was "meet by entrance when you can". Orange, however, meant "follow me now". Alice slipped out from behind the stall and hurried to catch up with him.

Claude led her through the pavilion to a tiny café tucked away in a corner by a stall that sold folded Polish dumplings called pierogi. They were doing a roaring trade, and so was the café. Every table was full to bursting with people talking animatedly at one another over steaming mugs of coffee and slabs of fruit cake. Alice was convinced that they would not find anywhere to sit, but as they moved through the packed café a table at the back miraculously cleared for them. The four men seated at it left their food untouched and headed back into the crowds. Their coffee was whisked away and fresh table linen was laid by a waitress who nodded conspiratorially at Claude. Alice raised an eyebrow.

"Welcome to HQ, Alice," Claude said, picking up the menu. "It has a perfect view of the pavilion's entrances and a cast-iron guarantee that nothing can ever be overheard."

"But anyone here could listen to anything we say," Alice objected. Even as she said it, she realised how ridiculous she was being. Everyone in the café must be one of their agents, or an ally. That was why the men had vacated this table and the waitress had known Claude.

Claude grinned. "I see you've worked it out already," he said. "There will always be space for you here, but you won't be able to get as much as an espresso without one of these."

He passed a small box across the table. Alice snatched it up and opened it. Inside was a small round pin with a wing etched into it in gold.

"Clip it under your collar," Claude said. "Don't let anyone see it unless you know they can be trusted entirely. Only people working on the Daedalus mission are allowed in here and anyone involved will know that you are someone who can be trusted. Talk to no one who doesn't have a pin." He paused. "Actually, to be on the safe side, talk to no one but me."

The words "trust no one" flashed into Alice's mind and she shook them away. That had been Uncle

Robert's advice and it was painful to remember it. In her last mission, on board the Sapphire Express, it had turned out to be horribly close to the truth.

Alice took the pin from the box and turned it in her palm so the light caught at the gold of the wing.

"The wings are for Daedalus," Claude said. "We're sure that whatever is going to happen is linked to those plans. Either that microfilm is going to be passed to the enemy or it already has been and they are plotting something even more terrible. Either way, it is linked to the Daedalus plane, somehow. The name just keeps cropping up. It can't be a coincidence."

"I'm ready to help," Alice said. "I've been here for three days. You haven't told me anything yet, so I haven't the faintest idea who I'm looking for and half the world has come to the fair. Haven't you been given *any* clues?"

Claude shrugged. "A couple of possible leads. There was one that I was very sure about but it turned out to be nothing – a pair of students from a university in Geneva. They were very interested in the pavilion where all the new plane technology is being exhibited and … well, I didn't like them."

"Why?" asked Alice.

Claude shrugged. "Oh, I don't know," he muttered irritably. "Too many photos, too many notes, too many questions. They just seemed so … so *keen*. There was just something *off* about them." He laughed. "I never did trust a man who wears bottle green."

"Maybe I could follow them…" started Alice, but Claude shook his head.

"No, there was nothing there after all. One of them is studying physics and the other is interested in aeronautics. Their records checked out. It was very annoying. That green suit."

He shuddered and Alice suppressed a laugh. Grown-ups got upset about the silliest things.

Claude leaned back in his chair.

"I have a task for you though, Alice. One of France's most talented engineers went missing yesterday. He was due at the Aviation pavilion to give a demonstration of his work on wing designs for biplanes, but he didn't arrive. His home has been emptied of everything."

"A kidnapping?" said Alice.

Claude nodded. "Possibly. He had knowledge

that would be valuable to the enemy, but we need to know if he has gone willingly or not. And there's something else. One of our agents has also disappeared. The same thing. The house empty as though she never lived there. She had been working on some enemy codes that they would be keen to keep from us, and she knows a great deal about France's airfields." His face fell. "Isabella. She was a good friend."

"So how can I help?" asked Alice

Was she imagining it, or did Claude look a little embarrassed at this? He waved at the waitress to let her know they were ready to order. Then he reached inside his jacket pocket and drew out a piece of paper.

"That's what I came to talk about," he said.

CHAPTER FOUR

"This isn't fair!"

Alice glared across the table at Claude. He glanced around and raised a hand to quiet her, but Alice was unstoppable.

"*I* got the information on that card! *I* tracked down the spy who was looking for it. *I* worked out the code. You can't shove me off on to some *babysitting* mission while you go and do the glamorous work. *Again!*"

"Alice—"

"Don't 'Alice' me. It's not fair and you know it."

Claude sighed.

"I would have thought a young girl like you would like to spend time at the Fashion pavilion. If you succeed in getting backstage, you'll be working with the most gorgeous frocks in the world." Claude clocked the look on Alice's face and changed tack. "We *need* you over there, Alice," he continued. "We're tracking every place that Isabella visited in the days before she went missing. We've done the same for Léo too – he's the missing engineer. One of the places Isabella visited on her last day was the fashion hall. And what's more, we found a scrap of paper in the room where the fashion shows are held with Léo's address on it. Someone in that pavilion knew where he lived and wrote it down, possibly to pass that knowledge on to others. It's not much to go on, but we have to try to find them, and to stop more people going missing. I know you were going to work on Daedalus with me, but plans change. We need someone who can listen out for gossip, spot any visitors who come back to the pavilion too often. Anything that might point to whether the fashion hall is linked to these disappearances."

"So someone else gets to track down the Daedalus plans?" Alice grumbled. This could have been her chance to prove how good a spy she was, and Claude was going to take the glory.

Claude leaned across the table towards her.

"Alice, remember the other night when you saved that girl on the boat? Remember what I told you? There is *nothing* more important than saving lives, Alice. Nothing. We need you in that pavilion."

Alice sighed. "All right," she said. "I'll try to think of a way to get backstage." She looked out across the crowds bustling through the hall and remembered the elegant young woman who had dashed over to their stand earlier that day.

"In fact, I think I may already have an idea."

Alice did not expect to see the young woman again so soon, but at eight o'clock, as they were closing their stand down for the evening, the girl in pink tweed made her way through the pavilion, waving a slip of paper in the air.

"Monsieur Fouray is a pet," she announced, sliding the deckle-edged card across the counter. "He says that you can come to one of the afternoon shows. The evening ones are all reserved. If you aren't posh enough to order an entire wardrobe, there's no way you can get into those, but the afternoon ones are a bit of a free-for-all. It's a chance for Paris to show itself off to the world, he says. The more the merrier."

Alice smiled. She was sure that her mother would allow her an hour or two away from their stall, but really she needed more than a ticket to the show.

"I don't suppose I could come backstage with you, could I?" she asked. "I bet it's so glamorous and exciting. I'd love to see what goes into making such a beautiful event."

The girl frowned. "Backstage? That's more secret

than my mum's duck pâté recipe that only comes out at Christmas," she said. "Everyone is so terrified of spies that no one gets backstage except for the make-up girls and us models."

"Spies?" Alice's ears had pricked up at the word.

"There are spies everywhere. Don't you read the gazettes? Last winter someone broke into Monsieur Fouray's workshop and copied down the designs of six of his dresses. Then they presented them at a show before *he* could. It was a huge scandal and now no one gets to see the centrepieces of his show till the moment they appear on the catwalk. Most of the show is repeated each day, but there is one dress in each show that is the 'look' of the day. Oh, hang on, that's not the right name for it. I wrote it down."

She emptied her purse on to the counter and pulled out a scrap of paper. "Here we go. Monsieur Fouray calls it his *Majesté du Jour*. It's the best frock for his poshest clients and it's a complete secret. Don't tell the other models I couldn't remember it. They all laugh at me as it is."

Alice relaxed. A fuss over a pretty frock was hardly the sort of spying she was interested in. Still, it was annoying that she would not be welcome backstage. She would have to think of another way.

"I will come tomorrow," she promised. "I'm Alice, by the way. Alice Éclair."

"Eva. I'm really Eva Castle. My mother's French but my dad's from England, so when I'm in a show I'm Eva Castillion. It's a bit more la-di-da. Oh, do come. I'm going to be in the centrepiece gown and if you are around afterwards, perhaps we could go for ices."

Alice assured her that she would love that. And as quickly as she had arrived, Eva was gone, dashing off towards the exit.

Alice slipped the ticket into her pocket and drew out her notebook. If she could not secure an invitation to backstage at the fashion show from Eva, she would just have to get one from Monsieur Fouray himself.

CHAPTER FIVE

The next morning, Alice rose early to start work. Madame Éclair had a long list of cakes and biscuits for her to complete for the fair but there was an added project that she needed to finish if she was to hope to get backstage at the fashion show. Progress was slowed by Casper, the cat from down the road, clawing at the door for treats every five minutes, and by Madame Éclair wanting to show off her new toy. The day before, she had wandered into the Innovations pavilion and had been persuaded to buy a new electric mixer with nine different blades and four speeds. It was ludicrously expensive and sat smugly in the middle of the counter at *Vive Comme L'Éclair*. Madame Éclair persuaded Alice to use it for mixing her cake, but whichever speed she tried and whichever blade she used, the awful thing would gum up and stop running. By 7a.m., Alice was ready to throw it into the river and had picked up her trusty wooden spoon and begun again, leaving the first batch of cake dough a sticky mess wrapped round the paddle in the thing's bowl.

While everything baked in the great Éclair oven, Alice looked over the sketches she had made late the night before and frowned. Would this work?

At nine o'clock the taxi arrived to take them across the city. Alice wound down the window and peered out at the crowds of visitors already bustling through the streets towards the fair. All of Paris was alive and she could feel the excitement in the air as the taxi sped through the crowded streets. The Tastes of the World pavilion was busier still and the morning passed in a whirl with Alice besieged by visitors eager to try her macarons, tarte tatins and profiteroles. It was almost three o'clock by the time she was able to escape and dash to the Fashion pavilion.

By the time she arrived, Alice had run through what she had to do a hundred times, terrified that she would get tongue-tied and nervous. Oh, why could she not be chic and confident like Claude? She had watched him charm everyone from theatre doormen to government ministers and he always knew what to say. She presented her ticket to the concierge at the door of the pavilion and was glad to see that he had a welcoming smile, quite unlike the snooty type that she had been expecting.

"Take a seat anywhere, Mam'selle," he said, passing her a slip of paper and a small pencil.

"Oh, except for the front tables. I'm afraid they are reserved."

Alice smiled back at him and walked into the pavilion. Her first impression was that she must have taken a wrong turn somewhere and found the Floristry and Gardening hall. There were flowers everywhere. Vases almost as tall as Alice stood around the room, overflowing with peach-coloured roses and long silky feathers that shimmered in the breeze coming through the arched windows. There were more flowers on the tables that filled the hall, and a single rose was tied with peach-coloured ribbon to the back of each of the chairs. The hall was already half filled with people sat at the tables, chattering excitedly with one another and pointing at anyone in the room who was particularly well dressed. Alice found a spare chair at a table close to the front, next to a long pink carpet that ran down the centre of the hall and up to a stage where a woman in a long gown was playing the harp. The other guests at the table were a mother with four impeccably dressed children and an elderly lady who turned from her conversation with them and quickly introduced herself as Madame Grenouille.

"Is this your first time at Monsieur Fouray's show, my dear?" the old lady asked Alice.

"Yes," Alice said, and because there was no reason not to tell the truth, she continued, "One of the models gave me a ticket yesterday. My mother has a stall in the Tastes of the World pavilion, the pâtisserie *Vive Comme L'Éclair*. I hope you will visit."

"A shop named after my favourite cake," said Madame Grenouille. "I will most certainly visit you."

"Well, it was named after my mother, really. Our name is Éclair, like the cake, but also like lightning. She named the shop 'Live Like Lightning' as a sort of joke."

"Be brave. Eat cake," the old lady chuckled. She smoothed her black crêpe dress down over her hips. She was what Alice's mother would call "a woman of generous circles", and was dressed top to toe in black, with a short, black silk veil half covering her face. Alice realised that she was in mourning dress, worn by people who had lost loved ones. It was not unusual to see women dressed in such a way in the city, especially in the years following the war. When Alice was tiny it felt as though half the world was dressed in black. But it was strange that Madame

49

Grenouille should go to a fashion show when she surely had no intent of buying any of the dresses for herself. And strange things were worthy of note.

Alice was about to ask her what her interest in the show was when the harp stopped playing and a man dressed in an exquisitely tailored suit walked through the curtains at the back of the stage and stood by a podium.

"Mesdames et Messieurs," he began, "it is my delight to welcome you to the viewing of my new collection, designed especially for this most illustrious gathering of nations. The theme is ... Paris and the World."

At this cue, the harp began to play. The models passed through the organza curtains at the back of the stage and paraded down the steps and along the carpet to the back of the hall, posing and smiling as they went. Alice strained her neck to see Eva, but could catch no sight of the friendly girl she had met in the hall.

"So inventive," murmured Madame Grenouille, as a girl dressed in a green gown on which were embroidered trellises of roses and honeysuckle flowers passed by their table. "And nothing like the designs of that upstart over there. Monsieur Fouray knows better than to pander to silly fashion."

Alice glanced over to where the old lady was pointing. At the side of the room sat a thin man in a bright-yellow suit wearing one pink shoe and one black. He was leaning back in his chair, glaring at everyone.

"That's Señor Rubio," she continued. "They say he is very popular in Spain but I stayed to watch his show once and it was *shocking*."

Alice wanted to ask how, but up on the stage Monsieur Fouray had begun to read from a folder set before him on the podium.

"Delphine is wearing *Tuileries la Nuit*. Pink and cream embroidery on this silk day dress celebrates our beautiful Tuileries Garden."

As dress after dress passed her, each with a story attached to it by Monsieur Fouray, Alice began to see that the fashion show was not just a parade of pretty frocks. It was a performance, a collection of images of how Monsieur Fouray experienced the beautiful city in which they lived. By the time Eva walked down the carpet dressed in a shimmering silver gown trimmed with sparkling diamanté, Alice was entranced. She was just craning her neck to see the detail on the front of the gown when she spotted the man in the bright-yellow suit lean down and pick up something from the floor as Eva passed by. It was very odd behaviour and reminded Alice that she was *meant* to be looking out for suspects and not enjoying the show quite so much.

"To close our show," Monsieur Fouray was saying, "Eva is wearing my gown of the day. As many of you know, our *Majesté du Jour* is revealed each day in our evening show, but tonight we have no evening show, so I have great delight in revealing it to you now. I present *Madame L'Eiffel*," Monsieur Fouray read, "a tribute to our beautiful *Dame de Fer*." Alice smiled. She had always loved the nickname that Paris gave the wonderful tower that had been built for the last World Fair. Eva looked wonderful. Gone was the slightly harried girl who had dashed across the pavilion's floor yesterday. In her place was a stately young woman with a straight back who seemed to glide across the floor, lit by the flashes from the photographers who were crowded into a group by the stage. As Eva passed Alice's table, she gave her a conspiratorial wink before settling her face back into a bland half-smile.

"Utterly charming, isn't she," whispered Madame Grenouille. "So like… Ah well, one must not look back." A shadow of sadness passed over the woman's face before she placed her slip of paper on the table and rose to her feet to applaud Monsieur Fouray. Alice noted that she had not placed a mark against any of the dresses listed on it. Once more, she wondered why this lady had come to the show.

Alice waited while the crowd of visitors gathered up their bags and left, chattering loudly about how beautiful everything they had just seen was. She saw a couple of ladies in more costly fashions pointing to items they had picked out on their slips of paper and talking to the young man by the counter, who leafed through a huge appointment book. Alice unclicked the clasp on her bag and took out two small boxes. She laid them gently on the table and opened them. The first contained eight lozenges of white chocolate she had prepared before leaving the shop and the second contained her precious piping cones. Working as quickly as she could, she drew out the lines of the dress Eva had been wearing on the first lozenge, picking out the sparkling hem and adding delicate curls of caramel chocolate around Eva's face to mimic her beautiful hair. With the merest hint of pink chocolate for her rosebud lips, the creation was complete. She moved to the next lozenge and, in moments, the pink and cream dress of the girl called Delphine appeared. By the time the crowds were beginning to thin to a handful of stragglers, Alice had recreated the entire show. She closed the lid on the box of chocolates, tied it with a satin ribbon, walked to the young man by the desk and presented it to him.

"My congratulations to Monsieur Fouray," she said, smiling. "Please make sure he gets these, with the compliments of pâtisserie *Vive Comme L'Éclair*. We are in the Tastes of the World pavilion."

Alice walked away smiling to herself. She would need to get back to the stall in good time for when Monsieur Fouray visited.

Because she was sure that he would.

CHAPTER
SIX

Less than half an hour later, the sprightly man in the impeccably cut suit arrived at the pâtisserie stall and asked for the young lady who had left such a generous gift at the Fashion pavilion. Alice hurried to greet him, eager to put the next part of her plan into action, but before she could introduce herself, he launched into a furious tirade.

"Mam'selle, are you determined to ruin me? I demand to know your price."

Alice frowned. This was not the reaction she had been anticipating. Monsieur Fouray continued, his voice rising as he waved his arms animatedly.

"Where did you get the designs from? I demand to know. The utmost security has been employed for this show and yet still you have managed to gain access to my designs. It is a scandal!"

For a moment, Alice was at a loss for words, but then she remembered what Eva had said about the secrecy that surrounded the dress designs. Did Monsieur Fouray think that she had seen the dress designs *before* the show?

"Monsieur, I created this *at* your wonderful show just this afternoon," Alice assured him. "I took the chocolate lozenges with me and decorated them after the show."

Monsieur Fouray paused, eyeing Alice warily as if trying to decide whether or not to believe her.

"How on earth could you do a thing like that so quickly? And why?" he demanded.

"To answer your first question: talent. And to answer your second: business, Monsieur," Alice said crisply, drawing herself upright and astounded at her own daring. "I present it as a business opportunity. I can come to your shows and create these on the spot. Something for your customers to take away to remind them of your beautiful designs. Available only on the day of the show and to a select few."

"Mam'selle is under the impression that Monsieur Fouray needs assistance to make an impression. Mam'selle is *greatly* misled," the man said frostily.

Alice paused. The lozenges had not been enough to convince him. She racked her brain to remember anything she had seen at the show that might help.

Of course.

Alice smiled softly and began to dust icing off the countertop. As if Monsieur Fouray were not there she murmured, "I will just have to accept Señor Rubio's offer then."

Monsieur Fouray's arm dashed out and caught at her wrist.

"What!" he cried. "That upstart! That pretender! That ... that ... *nobody*! No. I will not have this. Mam'selle, I offer you my great apologies. I thought you were one of those wicked rats come to steal my designs. I have many enemies, Mam'selle. They would stop at nothing, not even using a charming young lady such as yourself to steal my gowns for themselves. My gown of the season last spring – *Nocturne* – she was so beautiful. Peach organza with seed pearls and the finest silk cape. She was in no fewer than eleven shops on the very morning of my show. I tell you, Mam'selle, there are spies everywhere."

It took all of Alice's training to keep a straight face through this speech. There were, indeed, spies everywhere, but most of them were concerned with something rather more important than dress designs. She tried her best to look grave. She hoped that word would not get back to Señor Rubio about her deception, but that was unlikely. She had anticipated a little rivalry between the two, but from Monsieur Fouray's reaction it seemed almost as if it was outright war between the two designers. She really must ask Eva what was so shocking about the other's designs.

"To business, Mam'selle," Monsieur Fouray announced, clapping his hands. "I will employ you to come to my show once a day. You will sit backstage under the supervision of Monsieur Charles Deforges, one of my designers. You will not leave until every dress has been shown, and you will produce lozenges to be served with champagne while my guests discuss purchases."

Alice wanted to whoop with delight, but she forced herself to remain businesslike and tried to give the impression that she was giving Monsieur Fouray's suggestion serious thought.

"How many lozenges would you wish me to decorate?" she asked, taking an order book from the side of the counter.

"At each show I can have as many as fifty ladies," Monsieur Fouray said. "I would like you to attend in the evening, but tomorrow we have only one show, in the afternoon. Can you get away from your work here, do you think?"

Alice crossed her fingers behind her back

and nodded, hoping that she would be able to persuade her mother. It was a large order and all that decorating might keep Alice too busy to do any spying, but she *had* to get backstage. If only she was able to get a sneaky look at the dresses beforehand.

"It would help, Monsieur, if I were able to sketch your gowns ahead of time," she began, but Monsieur Fouray cut her off.

"Out of the question. It is my look of the day that I wish you to draw and that is not unveiled until the day of the show itself. You may see it when it first appears to my public and not one second before, and I warn you, Mam'selle, from the moment you see that gown you will not be out of Monsieur Deforges' sight. Do you understand?"

Alice nodded. The way that Monsieur Fouray behaved reminded her of how protective she was of her cake designs, but they were nothing compared to her precious notebooks. It really was the most ridiculous fuss over frills, ruffles and beading when people's very lives were at stake. Someone in that fashion hall had left Léo's address on a slip of paper the very day he disappeared, and then Isabella had gone missing. Had she been followed? It seemed that someone was sharing information far more important that Monsieur Fouray's frocks, and Alice was going to find out who.

Alice could not resist dashing to HQ to let Claude know how clever she had been. She left her mother flicking through a brochure called "Everything for the Modern Home" that she had picked up from a stall in the Innovations pavilion and made her way to the café on the edge of the hall. It was packed full as usual, and she waited until a couple who had given up hope of finding a seat were far enough away not to see her flash her pin badge at a woman near the entrance. Claude was sitting at a table at the back of the café, deep in conversation with a woman who looked near to tears. As Alice approached she heard the woman hiss, "We are running out of time."

"We're working on it, I promise," said Claude. "We are close to getting a spy inside the fashion hall and—"

"That *child!*" the woman spat back. "What use will she be!"

Alice felt her face flush. She almost did not want to hear how Claude would react. She was still not entirely sure that the older spy thought very much of her either.

"Alice is very skilled in spite of her age," Claude said. "A little headstrong sometimes, perhaps, but what she coped with on the Sapphire Express would have defeated many more experienced agents." He paused. "I trust her."

This was high praise indeed. Alice gasped, and Claude heard her.

"Alice," he cried. "Come and join us."

"No need, I'm going," muttered his companion, and she gathered her belongings together and hurried past Alice and out of the café. Claude sighed as Alice took her place, not sure how much she should admit to having overheard.

"She didn't mean to be rude," Claude said. "But she's very worried. So am I. We had word about Isabella."

Alice leaned forwards. "Has she been found?"

Claude frowned. "Not exactly, but at least we know she's alive. One of our operatives intercepted a communication that she and Léo will be moved out of the country on Friday. If we can track down whoever is giving away our spies' locations by then, we might be able to rescue them."

"But that's only three days away," said Alice.

"I know. But now you see why it's so important to get you into that pavilion. More important than the Daedalus plans. Nothing is more important—"

"Than a human life, I know. Don't worry – I've not only managed to get into the pavilion, they are allowing me backstage."

Alice waited to see if Claude was impressed, but he merely looked at her with impatience so she quickly filled him in on everything she had been doing.

"That all sounds very good, Alice," he said. "But you must be careful. Whatever you do, when you identify the spy, do not alert them. No heroics, please. Just find out who is passing the information and then let us know the instant you work it out. We don't want things being jeopardised by any foolhardiness. I've heard all about what happened on the Sapphire Express and we can't afford any mistakes."

Alice bristled. A few moments ago he had

been singing her praises to the woman who had questioned her ability. Now he was back to treating her like a child again. It was infuriating. She was about to object when she saw a shadow pass across Claude's face. Of course, he was worried about his friends. Alice bit back the smart remark that was on the tip of her tongue.

"I'll be able to keep an eye on everything that happens and I'll be really careful," she promised. "I start tomorrow."

CHAPTER SEVEN

"I can't think how you managed to persuade Monsieur Fouray to let you back here," Eva said. "You must be a witch or something."

Alice laughed. "I might have fibbed and said that Señor Rubio was interested in employing me," she confessed.

Eva's mouth dropped open. "Well, *that* would do it. They can't stand each other. You are clever."

It was the next afternoon and they were sitting backstage at Monsieur Fouray's fashion show, where Alice was putting her plan into action. Fifty chocolate lozenges lay in small piles in front of her and she was ready with her sketchbook for when the *Majesté du Jour* was unveiled. Persuading Madame Éclair had been easier than Alice feared.

"But of course you must go, Alice," her mother had said. "Working with one of Paris's fashion houses could be a good advertisement for us." So Alice had left her mother guarding the stall with only Casper, who had *somehow* crept into one of the cases that they had brought across the city that morning, for company. Casper was behaving very oddly lately, visiting *Vive Comme L'Éclair* even more than usual and following Alice around wherever she went. This was the first time that he had managed to get into the taxi with them though.

Eva nudged the chocolate squares with a bright-red nail.

"You can have one if you like," said Alice, airily pretending that she hadn't made five extra just in case they came in useful for making friends with the models.

"I shouldn't really," Eva admitted. "If I can't fit into the dresses I'll never get a job again. It's a horrid job is this one. Sometimes I think I'll give it all up and do something where no one cares what I look like in one of their silly frocks."

Before today, Alice would have been convinced that she was not serious. But backstage at the show was not quite as glamorous as she had imagined. Mostly everyone seemed to be in very bad moods with one another. In her head she had imagined that the models would be lounging on velvet, chatting to one another while trying on gorgeous frocks. She had thought it would be like the beautiful salon that she once visited while being fitted for a bridesmaid's dress. The shop owner had brought them all sparkling cordial and fussed over them while the bride picked out which shoes she wanted them all to wear and spent more time than Alice believed possible trying to decide between two identical shades of ribbon.

The fashion show was nothing like this. For a start, everything was crammed into a space about half the size of Alice's mother's shop. "The more space we take up, the fewer chairs they can fit into the hall," Eva had told her. "So here we are, the best-dressed sardines in Paris." It was true. What little space there was had been taken up by a rail that was hung with the most exquisite frocks that Alice had ever seen. They were guarded by Monsieur Fouray's designer, Charles Deforges, who had been appalled at Alice's presence. He had quizzed her about everything from her reason for being there to the contents of her pockets before grudgingly allowing her to squeeze her icing tools on to the tiny table where she was now sitting with Eva.

Everywhere she looked, the models were being buttoned into dresses while one of the team of young make-up girls and hairdressers pulled their hair into curling irons or applied nail lacquer. Everyone except Eva seemed to be doing about six jobs at once.

"I'm waiting for Jacqueline to be free," Eva explained. "My hair is instant frizz if it isn't done properly. No one except Jacqueline knows how to style it and Charles will kick up such a fuss if I walk down the steps looking like something the cat dragged in. He's only the assistant designer, but he acts as though it is *his* show rather than Monsieur Fouray's. And he's always changing stuff at the last minute. On Monday he almost *dragged* me off the runway to change the beading on my frock. I nearly broke my ankle. I've never worked with anyone so unprofessional."

Alice sneaked a look at Charles. He was examining the embroidery on the cuff of a burgundy frieze cloak and seemed to be picking at some of the stitches. She supposed that designers were just perfectionists. No wonder all the models looked a little harassed.

"Shouldn't you be icing the look of the day on to these?" asked Eva.

Alice shook her head. "I don't get to see it till you all do," she said. "Monsieur Fouray's orders. Charles seems to think that I'll try to sneak a look at it anyway. He keeps glaring at me. I don't think he trusts me."

Eva rolled her eyes. "Oh, ignore him. He's been in a foul mood all morning. My dress from yesterday was missing some of the beads. He's hopping mad because he says they were specially designed for it, and we can't find them anywhere. And Delphine's dress looks like it has had a piece hacked out of the back. She thinks it must have torn when she was talking with the guests after the show, but it's as if someone's taken a pair of scissors to it."

She sighed. "Anyway, Charles doesn't trust *anyone*. He sees spies everywhere. He thinks that they – oh, that's Jacqueline for me now." She leapt from the table and ran to join a harassed-looking young woman who was brandishing a curling iron and looked on the verge of tears.

Alice stared after her. What had she been about to say? She glanced over to where Charles was snipping at a flower bud sewn on to the pocket of a gown. Why had he been talking about spies with Eva? Alice decided that Charles was someone to keep a very close eye on.

Watching a fashion show from behind the scenes was much more exciting than watching it from the audience, Alice decided. To begin with, Monsieur Fouray had wanted her to wait at the back of the room to sketch the dresses, but after Alice had squeezed herself into a tiny space between the wall and a table full of shoe boxes, he had dashed through, grabbed her hand and dragged her to stand by the edge of the curtain, just out of sight. "You will watch the models make their entrance to the *gasps* of the crowd," he instructed. "My dresses are not static pictures. They are *alive! They sing! They breathe!* You need to see how they move." Monsieur Fouray was waving his hands around as he said this, his face full of animation. Then he dropped his hands to his side and looked at Alice sternly. "Just do not get in anyone's way."

This last instruction proved to be more difficult than she had thought, and Alice found that she was constantly jumping out of someone's way as they hurried towards the curtain, closely followed by a make-up girl waving a brush or by Charles making last-minute tweaks to the way that the dress draped. The minute they reached the curtain, however, they would become ethereal, all rush disappeared. They drifted through, barely looking out of breath, to circle the audience and pose at the edge of the stage while Monsieur Fouray described every fold of what they were wearing, and the photographers for Paris's fashion newspapers jostled to capture the image that would appear in the next morning's edition. Then they passed through the curtain again and turned once more into harassed-looking girls being hurried into another dress.

"Well, that's me done," said Eva, after her fourth turn of the hall. She was dressed in a duck egg blue tulle creation, all frills and flounces. She picked at one of its voluminous sleeves. "This thing looks gorgeous but it's so itchy, and I lost about four beads on the way round the hall. I think Charles has been snipping at the threads on them. I'd better change out of this and help Delphine get into today's centrepiece."

Alice's attention turned back to the show. Each time the curtain was pulled aside she took a good look at the audience. Madame Grenouille was there again, sitting at a table with a young couple who looked to be trying to ignore her constant chatter.

The hall was full of the same mix of people she had seen the day before, some examining the dresses for future purchases, others simply there for the show, not even bothering to mark down the names that Monsieur Fouray read out from his podium. There were even some that Alice recognised herself: one of the singers from the opera, and a woman who arrived, loudly and late, in a swathe of velvet and diamonds, and who Monsieur Fouray expertly paused the show for while she took her seat.

"That's Elisabet Aubert, the actress," hissed one of the models behind Alice's ear. "She never buys anything. She just wants to be seen at every show. She always buys from Señor Rubio. It would be quite a coup if Monsieur Fouray could steal her from him."

One man caught her eye. He was seated in the front row making careful marks on a slip of paper and every time he scribbled something down he fiddled nervously with the lapel of his suit. Alice half squinted and took a step closer to the curtain. It was the man who had smashed her model on the first day – the man who was so upset about losing a button! Was that something glinting next to the carnation in his buttonhole? She took another step.

"Mam'selle Éclair!" snapped Charles. "Your orders were to stay out of sight!"

Alice sprang back and narrowly avoided crashing into the table on which a pile of jewellery boxes was being stored, ready for their precious contents to be returned to the jeweller they had been borrowed from. This meant that as well as Charles being angry with her, the woman who was jealously guarding them was also now eying her suspiciously. Alice was halfway through a whispered apology while the woman checked to make sure that not a single earring had disappeared, when a strange hush fell over the backstage area. One of the models, Delphine, was moving towards the curtain, clad in what looked at first glance to be a shapeless cape, but which was actually a sheet draped round her shoulders to hide what was underneath. Monsieur Fouray's *Majesté du Jour* was about to be unveiled.

Alice leaned forwards. She would need to make sure that the lozenges she decorated looked as close to whatever was under the sheet as possible to impress Monsieur Fouray. She watched as Charles reached up to shake the sheet from Delphine's shoulders and heard a ripple of delight as the dress was revealed. It was a concoction of organza that shimmered in the light. Cream at the shoulders, where diamantés glistened against Delphine's delicate shoulders, and then melting into peaches and pinks in the cascades of fabric that fell from the waistline into a froth of blue around her heels. Alice picked up the pencil she had left on the table, ready to sketch as Delphine walked out into the hall. She must catch the movement of the frock perfectly. The curtain was pulled aside and she heard the gasp of the audience. Her pencil rested against the slip of paper in her hand. Alice edged closer to the curtain's edge and looked out across the room.

At the back of the hall, away from the adoring crowd and the gathering press, stood two young men. One of them was making hurried notes in a small notebook, but that was not what caught her eye. The taller of the two was dressed in a suit of bottle green.

CHAPTER EIGHT

Alice was only barely aware of the next few minutes, of the crowd outside breaking into applause, of Delphine sweeping through the curtain in triumph to be met by more applause from her fellow models. Her mind was racing. She was sure that the two men were the engineering students that Claude had mentioned. They were in the Fashion pavilion. Did that mean that his initial suspicions had been correct after all? But if that were so then did that mean the Daedalus plans and the disappearances were somehow connected? Claude had talked about them as though they were two separate missions.

She was shaken out of her thoughts by Delphine. As soon as the model stepped through the curtains she gave a little cry of alarm and grabbed at the table on which lay the lozenges that Alice was to decorate.

"What on earth!" Delphine cried out. "What are all these tiny *balls* doing on the floor? I could have broken an ankle!"

Alice glanced at the floor. Lost in thought, she had knocked over a pot of tiny shimmering sugar balls that she had brought in case they were needed for decoration. They ran hither and thither across the

77

floor, making the other models shriek as they tried to step out of their way, for fear of stepping on them and falling too.

"I'm so *sorry*," Alice cried. "I'll get a brush and sweep them up." She looked around frantically for a broom, but one of the make-up girls took her by the elbow.

"I will do it, Mam'selle," she said. "I know where everything is."

Alice stared after her gratefully as the models, shooting her slightly reproachful looks and taking dainty steps to try to avoid falling on the slippery floor, made their way to their dressing tables.

She sighed. This was not a great start to her work at the fashion show. She would need to impress Monsieur Fouray very well in order to make sure she was not ejected on the first day. She turned back to the table and picked up her icing cones.

Half an hour later Alice sat in front of fifty white chocolate lozenges, each with Delphine's dress, *Joie du Printemps*, sketched out in pink chocolate. She had added a wash of blue and peach colouring over the outline, and flecks of chocolate around the hem gave the image a sense of movement as Delphine's heels kicked up the froth of the skirt. She had steeled herself to concentrate and it had taken every ounce of determination not to dash out into the hall and follow the two students. But it would do her no good to let Monsieur Fouray down and lose her chance to be so close to everything that was going on. If the spies really were passing information from the fashion hall, then that is where she needed to be.

"Perfect, Mam'selle Éclair," Monsieur Fouray declared, motioning to two young assistants to collect up the lozenges on to silver trays. "You see how wise you were to choose to work with me and not that imposter, Rubio! I am so glad that you did not give him a second thought." Alice smiled to herself. This was not quite how she remembered their first meeting.

Monsieur Fouray beckoned for Alice to follow him and they walked out into the hall where well-dressed ladies were milling around, chatting animatedly and sipping from sparkling glasses. The young man who had greeted Alice the day before wandered through the small crowd with a leather-bound book, moving from group to group and making notes with a silver pencil. As Monsieur Fouray approached them, the assembly broke out into polite applause and murmurings of "beautiful, Monsieur" and "your finest yet" could be heard. One lady grasped his arm and blurted out, "I simply *must* have *Joie du Printemps* for my daughter's twenty-first birthday next month." Monsieur Fouray smiled at her and gently passed her on to the man with the notebook who, Alice supposed, was making the necessary appointments.

"We have a surprise treat for you today, ladies. A taste of Fouray's to take home with you – *Joie du Printemps, au chocolat!*"

The lozenges, with Alice's beautiful piping, were brought forward and there were exclamations of delight over the detail. She was the centre of attention for a few minutes as the ladies crowded round her. Then they drifted back to their conversations and gently battled with one another to secure the earliest date possible for an appointment. The only person who did not appear to be impressed was Señor Rubio, who stood at the back whispering into the ear of the actress Elisabet

Aubert. As the crowd around Alice began to thin, he walked forwards, took one of the lozenges between his fingers and scowled.

"*Joie du Printemps*, you say, Mam'selle," he scoffed. "Let me show you a true *Majesté du Jour.*" He dropped the chocolate back on to the plate, whisked open his notebook and made a quick sketch of the beautiful gown that Delphine had worn. Then, in a few brief strokes, it had become something else. The organza was bunched into a great cloud at the neck. The billowing hem had been slashed. The diamantés were no longer delicately strung at the shoulder but criss-crossed the model's face. It was grotesque and alarming but at the same time it was beautiful. Before she could stop herself, Alice gasped.

"It's wonderful."

The man snapped the notebook shut.

"You're not the only one who can draw, Mam'selle. But this … frippery … is from a dying age. Monsieur Fouray is stuck in the past. Perhaps you should find something more modern to paint."

And with that, he turned on his heels and left.

Alice felt rather shaken. She had not expected the

world of fashion to involve quite such bitter rivalry.

That's not what you're here for, she reminded herself. She scanned the room, but there was no sign of the two students she had seen earlier. She checked the clock that hung at the back of the hall. Her mother was not expecting her back at the stall today so perhaps she could go looking for them. The Aviation pavilion should be her first port of call. If the disappearances really *were* linked to the Daedalus plans somehow, they may have gone back there. And if she could prove there was a link, then maybe Claude would let her be more involved in the Daedalus plot after all. She waved a quick goodbye to Eva and slipped out of the hall.

Alice hurried through the rest of the Fashion pavilion, past a stall hung with silks from China in every colour of the rainbow and a display from Italy of cashmere wraps and leather handbags. She passed a man in a kilt and checked shawl who was performing a dance comprised mainly of whirls and kicks to a group of tourists, and a stall where a woman was spinning wool on a wheel, her fingers deftly turning the fluffy fleece into a strong cream thread.

"Excuse me," cried a voice behind her, and Alice turned around too late to stop someone in khaki trousers and a grimy shirt colliding with her, hurling her to the ground.

"Urgh, I'm sorry. I'm in a rush!" A girl who looked a little older than Alice leaned over her, holding out a hand, but Alice saw how much oil there was on it and shook her head. She hauled herself up and dusted herself down. How infuriating. This was her best suit and there would be no time to clean it before she was needed at Monsieur Fouray's tomorrow. She looked angrily at the girl. Why hadn't she been watching where she was going?

"I really am sorry," the girl said. She took a handkerchief out of her pocket and wiped her fingers on it before holding her hand out to Alice again. "I'm Sophie. I was running to catch the land train to the Aviation pavilion, but I guess I'll just have to wait for the next one now."

Alice found her interest piqued at the mention of the Aviation pavilion but also, if she was honest, at the land train. On the way into the fair in the morning she had spotted the small series of linked carriages that wove their way through the site so that tourists could avoid walking or could just take in the whole site without pushing their way through the crowds. It looked fun, but she had not yet had any reason to use it.

"You didn't tear anything, did you?" asked Sophie. "I'm more used to cogs and wiring, but I'm not bad with a needle and thread either."

Alice shook her head. "I think it's just dust. I hope it comes out before tomorrow though. I'm working over at the Fouray show. I can't get away with looking like a ragamuffin."

Sophie laughed. "Like me, you mean? I'm usually at the Aviation pavilion. I'm not sure that the fashionable ladies are very comfortable having me around here."

Alice laughed. Sophie's outfit *was* drawing a few alarmed looks, especially given how much grease there was on it. She wondered what on earth had brought the girl to a pavilion full of expensive silks and the very latest fashions. As if reading her mind, Sophie drew a roll of thick woven ribbon out of her pocket.

"The strongest webbing in the world," she said. "I ran out this morning and I'm halfway through—

Well, that I can't tell you. It's a surprise for the last day of the fair."

Alice raised an eyebrow. First Monsieur Fouray and his fashion spies and now here was a girl from the Aviation pavilion with top-secret plans. Everyone at the fair seemed to be hiding something.

"I was going to the Aviation pavilion myself," Alice said. "I don't suppose you'd show me where it is, would you? I haven't really explored yet."

Sophie nodded. "If you like planes I could show you round my workshop. Papa is a mechanic and I want to build planes when I'm older. I want to be like Raymonde de Laroche. Everyone remembers her for her flying, but did you know she was an engineer?"

Alice didn't, but she was sure that by the time they reached the Aviation pavilion she would know all about France's pioneering pilot. Sophie was clearly just warming up to her favourite subject of conversation.

They stepped out into the afternoon crowds. The Fashion pavilion was surrounded by halls dedicated to other arts, and tourists could be seen flooding in and out of exhibitions of stained glass, ceramics and woodworking. Across the road, through a tree-lined avenue, she could see crowds waiting their turn to go into the Jewellery pavilion. Sophie motioned towards the ceramics exhibition, where a squat, open-topped car was waiting, pulling four box-shaped carriages, each large enough for two couples facing one another.

"Quick," said Sophie, grabbing Alice's arm. They made a dash for the final carriage and piled in. A few minutes later the train gave a shudder and moved off. Alice looked out at the fair as they drew past the grand pavilions built to showcase each of the nations of the world. Ahead of them, Alice could see the curved front of a building that looked like a huge birdcage of wire and glass. The afternoon sun glinted off it, illuminating the machines that hung from the roof inside like enormous birds. Alice gasped.

"Some of the best planes in France," Sophie laughed. "Aren't they beautiful? One of them is ours but you can't see her from here. We're tucked away at the back. Come on, this is our stop. Welcome to the *Palais de l'Air.*"

CHAPTER
NINE

The Palace of the Air was as much about space and light as the Fashion pavilion had been about crowds and colours. It was a great open hall with polished marble floors that reflected the smooth shapes and shining silver tones of the aircraft that were dotted around it, each one surrounded by people jostling to be the next on to the viewing platforms for a glimpse of their plush interiors. In the middle of the room was a small plane roped off with velvet and standing on a red carpet. A perfectly coiffured woman in a crisp blue jacket and skirt was handing out glossy brochures and gushing about "the wonders of modern flight."

"That's the Golden Kite," Sophie said. "The absolute height of luxury in flying. It's tiny, really, just enough room inside for two people and an air hostess, but it's supposed to be the most comfortable way to fly. The company who own it are hoping to sell it to Europe's richest families. The bigger planes over there are for passengers like us. Everyone who's anyone wants to fly nowadays. Papa says that's a great opportunity if you're an engineer. I just love how it feels to be up in the air."

Alice looked upwards to the roof, a great expanse

of glass from which were suspended balloons with passenger baskets slung beneath, and an enormous aeroplane, tilted as if in flight.

"That's Elise," Sophie said. "I insisted on naming her after Raymonde, of course. Elise was her first name. Papa built her, but he let me help, and the new project I'm working on is all my own creation."

Alice was only half listening. Part of her was marvelling at how beautiful the space was. She had never flown, but she longed to know what it was like to be up above the world, looking down, as if she had wings of her own. She was so entranced that she nearly walked into the middle of a group being given a lecture by a bespectacled woman.

"There's Papa," Sophie exclaimed. The introduction was unnecessary. The man in overalls striding towards them was unmistakably related to Sophie. He had the same broad grin and hazel eyes.

"Sophie, you have made a friend," the man said, holding out his hand. Like Sophie's, it was smeared with grease and only just in time did he remember to wipe it on a handkerchief.

"This is Alice, Papa. We met at the Fashion pavilion," said Sophie.

Sophie's father smiled a broad smile. He had kind eyes, Alice decided, and the way that he beamed at Sophie made it clear how proud he was of her. "Henri Alain at your service, Mam'selle," he said. He looked down at his hands. "I am afraid we are usually covered in oil of some kind."

"We're only allowed to be in the pavilion because Papa agreed to help out with other people's planes as well as our own," Sophie said. "It keeps him very busy, but if someone sees how great our planes are, we'll be—"

"As rich as Croesus!" her father exclaimed.

"A very old, very rich king," Sophie explained. "Papa is *obsessed* with history. Don't let him start on old myths or we'll be here for ages. He's already dragged me round the art exhibitions to look at all the pictures of Icarus and Hercules and whatnot."

Sophie's father frowned at her, but in a playful way that made Alice laugh.

"I'm usually covered in flour," admitted Alice.

"At the Fashion pavilion?"

Alice laughed. "I usually work as a pâtissière. I have been making chocolate lozenges for the fashion shows. Well, my first today, but I hope to make more."

Sophie nodded politely, but Alice could tell she was not very impressed. She supposed that icing pictures on to chocolate slabs was not very exciting to someone who built flying machines. Her father was more enthusiastic.

"Wonderful," he exclaimed. "Such artistry. A good *mille-feuille* contains the sort of attention to detail required to keep one of these beasts safely in the air. They taste rather good too."

Alice laughed. "They are one of my specialities," she said. "I must try to bring some over to you."

Monsieur Alain spread his arms out in delight. "Then we must pay you back in some way. Would you like to see inside our pride and joy?" He pointed up to the roof, where a large biplane hovered, and Alice blanched a little.

"I've … I've never been in a plane," she said.

"No need to fear, my dear. There is a walkway over her wing."

Ten minutes later, Alice was standing on a steel walkway looking down on to the wing of the aircraft high above the floor of the hall. The visitors, so tiny from up here, milled around like dropped raisins. Sophie had clipped herself into a sturdy harness and climbed into the cockpit of the plane, where she was showing off all the controls to Alice.

"I wish we could take her out," she said, flipping switches and pushing a stick that made flaps on the back of the wing spring up. "She flies like a dream. Almost as well as I'm sure Ariadne will fly."

"Sophie…" Monsieur Alain began. Alice heard a warning in his voice, but why? *Who was Ariadne and why was she to be kept a secret?*

"Oh, don't be daft, Papa. I can tell Alice. I'm pretty sure she isn't a spy."

Alice gulped and hoped the hot flush that had suddenly spread through her body had not reached her face. She tried to look as though she was deeply interested in the sleek machine in front of her. But Sophie was too engrossed in pretending to fly to notice Alice's embarrassment. Her father coughed gently and raised an eyebrow and, with a sigh, Sophie reluctantly climbed out of the cockpit, making the plane sway in an alarming manner and clatter against the walkway. Alice marvelled at how confidently the girl leapt from the plane to the safety of the walkway, then she unclipped herself from the harness and joined them.

"All right," she said. "We'll let you get back to work. I'm going to introduce Alice to Ariadne." She turned to Alice, her face suddenly serious. "But you have to swear on something appropriately serious that you won't tell *anyone* about this."

Alice thought for a moment. "May my soufflés never rise again if I break your trust," she said, holding out her hand.

"Come on then, this way. Are you coming, Papa?"

Monsieur Alain shook his head. He was looking down into the hall, waving at someone.

"Victor and Paul are here," he said. "I promised I'd talk them through wing aerodynamics."

Alice was instantly alert and turned her head to follow Monsieur Alain's gaze. Claude had mentioned two students who were hanging around the aviation hall. Perhaps Victor and Paul were the men he had mentioned. He had dismissed them as innocent, but still, she wanted to see what they looked like. However, Sophie rolled her eyes, grabbed Alice by the arm and dragged her along the walkway towards a ladder that led still further up to the roof of the building. The thought of scaling it made Alice gasp, but Sophie was up it in an instant and disappeared through a hatch above them. Alice followed more cautiously, making sure that her hand was wrapped securely round each rung before lifting her feet, and determined not to look down into the cavernous hall beneath her. Reaching the top, she clambered out and on to the roof of the building, where Sophie stood next to a tiny plane, barely taller than she was. It was entirely made of wood, painted red, except for the propellor, and with a silver streak down the side.

"Alice, meet Ariadne," she said.

Alice stared at the tiny plane.

"Did you build this?" she asked.

Sophie nodded. "'Finest engineer of her generation' – that's what Papa says about me. It's little more than a glider really, with just the tiniest engine, but I have engineered the wings for extra control and it can travel further than any glider with just a little help from the prop. Sorry, the propellor," she added, seeing Alice's confused expression. "I'm building her up here so that I can fly her. All the ones in the hall are just for show. I mean, they

94

can fly, they're just not going to this week. But I want to show off Ariadne. Papa and I really need a break. He's so talented, but none of the big flight companies will hire him. They all want younger men straight out of the big universities, and Papa taught himself. He knows far more than those students he likes to talk to. They're learning more from *him* than he is from them." She looked embarrassed. "He's funded everything we've built himself. Truth is, we're running out of money and I don't want him to give up and go back to working in a factory. We need to make a big splash, so I'm going to launch her on the last night of the fair and fly her down towards the Chaillot Palace. There's a huge air show planned, with balloons and small aeroplanes, all lit up and floating over Paris. I'm not invited, of course, but if I take part anyway then no one will be able to ignore us!"

Alice's eyes widened. "But that's all the way down at the other end of the fair," she said. "You'll have to cross the river."

From the roof they could see the entire fair spread out beneath them – the smart new buildings of the national pavilions, and the great exhibition halls with their banners and wide windows. To the north, the Eiffel Tower rose above them, festooned with fluorescent tubes that would light it up like a beacon when night fell. To the south, across the river, she could see the two biggest national pavilions, Germany's and Russia's, facing one another across the square that led to the Chaillot Palace, and the palace itself, a great curve, designed to show off the very best of France's architecture and house her great science exhibitions.

"Oh, just you wait," grinned Sophie. "She'll go further than you imagine. I wish I could take her out now and show you how amazing she is. Tell you what, come back tonight and maybe we'll take a night flight."

Alice stared. She had never been in a plane. It was a terrifying thought. Then again, it might be useful to spend more time with Sophie. And besides that, Sophie's words had reminded Alice why she was here. The Daedalus was meant to fly further than any other plane could. Did Sophie know anything about that? She tried to shake the thought. After all, how could Sophie be a spy? She was only a girl.

But then again, thought Alice, *so am I.*

CHAPTER
TEN

Alice hurried along the riverbank, glancing anxiously at her wristwatch. She was late for her meeting with Claude. Preparing the blank lozenges for the next day's show had taken longer than she'd expected, and she had also started work on a secret project, something that she hoped would impress Monsieur Fouray enough to keep her working at the shows. By the time she reached their meeting place by Pont de l'Alma, he was already beginning to pace up and down.

"Sorry," she muttered, falling into place beside him and pretending to be engrossed in one of the boat parades that were put on for fair visitors and tourists. The bigger crowds were near the tower and the beautiful church of Sainte-Chappelle, so they could talk freely, but as she had once been told, "you never know who is listening". The words popped into Alice's mind before she could stop them and she shuddered. It was Uncle Robert who had said that and she did not like to think of him. It was too upsetting.

"Well, you're here now," said Claude with none of his usual friendly charm. "Tell me everything that happened in the fashion hall."

"I was backstage for most of it, but I managed to get into the audience for a little while. There is a woman who was at today's show *and* the one I was at yesterday. She's called Madame Grenouille. She goes to them all, apparently, and she talks to everyone. She might just be a bit of a gossip, I suppose, but – well, you do always say to take an interest in nosy people."

"And you suspect something?"

"No. Well, yes. She has no intention of buying anything. Why go?"

Claude shrugged. "She doesn't sound very likely, but, as you say, you never know. Anything else?"

"There's a man who sits in the front row. He takes a *lot* of notes, and he fiddles with a badge on his lapel. I can't get close enough to see what is on it though. Do you think it might be a Daedalus pin? We don't have any other spies at the fashion show, do we?"

"No, especially none foolish enough to wear their pin on the outside of their lapel! Some of the enemy's spy rings have insignia though. I could get you drawings of them. Did you see him talk to anyone?"

Alice shook her head. "He left pretty quickly after the show finished, from what I could see."

Claude glanced at the river as a float passed by full of girls dressed in peach and pink organza dresses, dancing round brightly coloured mushrooms. Each float was a different vision of "Fairyland" and most of them were similarly bright and frothy.

"Just look at this utter nonsense," scoffed Claude.

Alice followed his gaze, glad of the distraction. Claude was on edge. It struck her that it must be frustrating for him, sitting on the sidelines while she tried to find the spy who was betraying his friends. She had thought at first that he had palmed her off on something minor while he went after the more important Daedalus plans, but now she saw that it must be torture for him to not be involved in a mission that might save people who were important to him.

"Claude," Alice said, almost not wanting to ask. "Why did you send me to the fashion hall? Why not go yourself?"

Claude sighed. "If I thought I could have done it myself I would have done," he said. "But you are the best person for this job. You are very good at getting people to talk to you, Alice. I knew I had to take a step back. But please understand – that was hard."

Alice nodded.

"I'll find them," she said.

A glow from under the bridge showed another float was approaching. It was Fairyland as the Ice Queen might have imagined it, a glittering display of ice-white crystal. Shards of carved, melting ice surrounded a throne of glass on which sat a woman in a white velvet gown, trimmed with silver. She held a glass sceptre topped with sparkling diamonds and her hair was piled high on her head, threaded through with strands of silver and gemstone clips. Alice gasped at how beautiful she looked. As the float passed, the woman caught Alice's eye and winked.

"Eva!" Alice cried. "Oh, doesn't she look gorgeous! She's one of the models at the fashion show."

Claude watched the float go by but it barely seemed to register with him. His mind was clearly elsewhere.

"Alice, now that you know why I stepped back

from your mission I need to ask you again to step back from mine. I know that you went to the Palais de l'Air after the show."

Alice bit her lip. "You spotted me!"

"You can't seriously expect to go to the one place we are investigating without being noticed." His face was serious. "But we talked about this, Alice. You are to stay out of the Daedalus investigation. We need you keeping an eye on things over in the Fashion pavilion. Isabella and Léo are depending on us. And there's more. An attempt was made against another of our agents tonight. They didn't succeed in taking her, but she is pretty shaken up by it. Somehow, between yesterday and today, her position was passed to the enemy."

Alice nodded. "I won't let you down, I promise. I only went to aviation because – well, I saw those two men you mentioned. They were at the fashion show. So I went to see if they would be at the Aviation pavilion and that's when I met Sophie and her father."

Claude frowned. "Alice, I told you, I don't think those two students have anything to do with this. You mustn't let yourself get distracted. It was a red herring. No, I've been watching quite a different quarry. There is a steward at the Aviation pavilion. She is in charge of showing people round that ridiculous Golden Kite."

"Why ridiculous?" asked Alice.

A look of irritation flashed across Claude's face. "Well, just look at it!" he snapped. "All round Europe people are worried that there could be another war, even more deadly than the last. Engineers are trying to work out how to build better machines to protect their countries and what do the owners of that piece of frippery do? They build a luxury plane only good for transporting a handful of spoiled socialites."

"But why suspect *her*?"

"Think about it, Alice. She is at the centre of that hall every day, watching who comes in and goes out. She is handing out pamphlets to everyone who comes to look at that absurd machine. Who knows what else might be handed over to her, or by her? She's a much more likely suspect than those two boys you keep going on about."

Alice blushed and fell silent. After a few moments Claude let out a great sigh.

"Well, you may as well tell me what happened

once you were there. There might be something of use."

"I didn't see them," Alice said in a small voice. She felt foolish for having wasted precious time chasing shadows and she hated feeling that she had let Claude down. "I met Sophie – Sophie Alain, that is. She's an engineer, and so is her father, Monsieur Alain. He's helping out with a lot of the machines at the pavilion, but no one wants to hire him because he's old."

She thought for a second. It felt disloyal to cast any doubt on Monsieur Alain, but Claude was making her feel very guilty. She did not want to hide anything from him.

"There was one odd thing," she said. "Sophie is so talented. A genius really. She has built a plane by herself – a glider that can glide further without power than any other plane before. It's incredible, but somehow I got the feeling that her father doesn't like her talking about her work. He's almost as secretive as you are and I don't know why. Why would he want to hide things when he wants their work to get noticed so that some big aeronautics firm will hire him? It doesn't make sense. We didn't speak for long though. He had visitors."

"And who were they?"

"I didn't see," Alice said. "He just called down to them, but Sophie dragged me away before I could look at them. He called their names, though – Victor and Paul, he said."

"Oh," said Claude. "But those *are* the students I told you about. Victor and Paul."

"So they *might* be involved."

Claude rolled his eyes. "Alice, stop. They're just boys."

And I'm just a girl, thought Alice. Typical of Claude. She was about to object but what Claude said next pushed all thought of Victor and Paul out of her mind.

"Your Monsieur Alain, on the other hand; he sounds interesting. I never trust secretive people. Maybe I should keep a closer eye on him."

"But—" Alice stopped herself. She had been about to say, "But he's nice," and she realised how ridiculous that would sound. But surely Monsieur Alain could not be mixed up in any of this?

"I'm not going to call you into the Daedalus investigation, Alice, but if there is a link to your new friends – well, you might be helpful. But I need your promise that the fashion show will be your primary focus. We can't afford to lose any more people and we *must* find Isabella and Léo before they are taken across the border. I will keep an eye on Monsieur Alain and ask around about him, but perhaps you should spend more time with this Sophie. The fashion halls aren't open *all* the time – spend your free time with her."

"She invited me to go flying in her plane this evening," Alice said, feeling miserable at the thought of spying on her friend.

Claude jumped up from his seat, snatched Alice's jacket from the back of her chair and almost threw it at her.

"Then what are you waiting for? Get over there at once."

Alice got up.

It felt wrong to be spying on her friend, but what if Claude was right? What if Monsieur Alain *was* involved somehow?

Worse still, what if Sophie was?

CHAPTER ELEVEN

By the time Alice reached the Palais de l'Air she felt extremely uncomfortable, and Sophie's broad smile as she climbed the walkway to greet her made her feel even worse.

"You came! Oh, I'm so glad," Sophie cried, wiping her hands on a rag, which did little to help with how dirty they were. "And you brought a friend."

Alice stared at her. What on earth did she mean? The answer to this was a meow from behind her.

Alice rounded on the cat.

"Casper! Oh, you dratted animal. I had to pass home to get here and he must have followed me," she explained to Sophie. "He's acting very strangely lately, following us everywhere. He's not even my cat!"

"I don't think anyone ever owns a cat," said Sophie. "They own us. Well, bring him up and I'll see if I can find him a salmon paste sandwich."

Alice glared at the cat as she hauled him, complaining, into her arms.

Monsieur Alain leaned out of the Golden Kite that sat gleaming under spotlights in the middle of the pavilion and waved up at them. Alice was reminded of what Claude had said. Could the smiling woman in the smart costume really be one of the spies? It did not seem very likely to her.

"Ah, you've come to keep Sophie company," called Monsieur Alain. "I have to work late tonight and I don't want her getting into any trouble."

Sophie winked at Alice and leaned close to her ear. "Papa will be busy for ages," she whispered. "The Golden Kite is meant to be having an exhibition flight at the end of the fair so they want him to check over all her controls. We can sneak Ariadne out and be back before he notices we're gone."

"But she's a glider," said Alice. "How will you get her back on to the roof?"

"She's *mostly* meant for gliding," said Sophie. "But, like I said, she has a tiny engine. I'll use the prop to get some lift and then we can glide back on to the roof. There's plenty of space. Don't worry. Just don't tell Papa. *No one* worries like he does. You know what parents are like."

Alice suppressed a smile. If Madame Éclair had any idea of the sort of danger Alice got herself into, she would be in big trouble.

Sophie led her to the stepladder, which was very difficult to climb with a wriggling beast on her shoulder, and they made their way to the roof. In the moonlight the plane's red paint gleamed like a ruby. Beyond the edge of the roof, the city's lights displayed Paris as if it were a glittering map. Alice walked to the parapet and peered over and down into the streets below; the lights of motor cars sparkled like tiny grains of sugar,

"Um... Are you sure this is safe?" she asked.

Behind her, Sophie laughed. "Flight's never safe, but she's safer than most and I'm an excellent pilot, honest," she said. "We'll just go round once. Get in the front."

Alice stared at her. "But I don't know how to fly this," she said, aghast.

Sophie laughed. "The front seat is for passengers. I'll fly from the back seat. But I'll show you the controls. I'm really proud of how well I've positioned them. I think a beginner could fly Ariadne – not that we're going to try that out tonight," she finished, noticing Alice's terrified expression.

Sophie hauled herself up into the back seat of the tiny plane and started to check through all the controls inside. Alice watched with fascination as she ran through the tiny pump that sent fuel into the little plane's engine and used levers to keep it going. There was a large stick to move the wings so that the plane could rise and turn, and a handful of dials showing how high they were and how much fuel they had. It seemed less complex than she had feared, certainly less so than that infernal mixing machine that Madame Éclair had brought back from the Innovations pavilion.

"Get in," said Sophie. "I've got to start the propeller and pull away the chocks that are holding the wheels in place. They're on levers for a quick getaway."

Alice placed Casper on the ground and gave him strict instructions to "stay". Then she clambered into the front seat of the plane and scrabbled for the seatbelt. Sophie jumped out and went to the front of the plane and in moments the propeller was spinning. Then she climbed back in, leaned out to pull on a lever and the plane jolted forwards. Alice held her breath as it rolled towards the edge of the roof. The plane was beginning to tip when, with a single leap, Casper jumped from his safe spot on the roof into Alice's lap. She cried out, but it was too late to put him back. The plane rolled forwards...

And they were falling.

Alice was sure her heart had stopped. The blood pounded in her ears. She was barely aware of Sophie behind her working the controls, and the wings creaking as they tilted in response. All she could focus on was the ground rushing to meet them, the wind blasting her face, and Casper digging his claws into her arms and yowling with alarm. And then she felt the plane right itself and they were climbing, pulling away from the ground and up into the night sky, Sophie carefully shifting the wings so that they caught the air. Alice peered tentatively over the side and saw the roofs of the pavilions passing below, almost close enough to touch. She had never seen the city from this angle before. She craned her neck to try to see *Vive Comme L'Éclair* in its tiny street on the outskirts, but there were too many taller buildings in the way.

Alice's stomach had stopped reeling and she was beginning to enjoy herself, even if Casper wasn't. She held him close and whispered comforting "shh" sounds into his ear. She looked out over the city, and the bells of Notre-Dame began to chime the hour.

"Sophie, it's nine o'clock!" she cried.

"And?"

"They will be starting the firework show by the tower. Are we high enough to be safe?"

As if to answer, Sophie took the plane further up and they soared over the city. As the last chimes of the bells began to fade away, the night sky exploded with colour. Alice ducked as a rocket whizzed past her ear. Casper began to yowl again.

"That one was a bit rogue," cried Sophie. "Oh, my gosh, Alice, why did you bring the cat with you!"

"I didn't! But like you said, cats go wherever they want to, the nuisance things."

"Well, let's take Ariadne home," said Sophie as another rocket whooshed past them. "I don't want her to get hurt."

Alice was about to shout "You mean damaged" but she wasn't entirely sure that Sophie did mean damaged. She seemed to treat Ariadne like a family member. They tipped sideways as Sophie expertly let the plane bank to the left and then they were heading back to the Palais de l'Air. Alice felt Ariadne judder again as Sophie turned off the propeller and they dropped suddenly before once again settling into a glide. The roof of the pavilion was rising to meet them and Alice was sure that they were going to crash, but Sophie pulled back on the controls and, with a few flicks of the wings, they slowed, touched down on the roof and skidded into place barely a metre from the edge. Sophie jumped out and dragged two heavy-looking blocks of wood to the plane, wedged them under the tyres and helped Alice get back down to the ground. Casper leapt out behind them, stretched and then began to calmly lick his paws as if he hadn't just spent five minutes yowling his head off with fright.

"Sophie, that was incredible!" Alice gasped. "Ariadne is amazing. How did you manage to create something so ... so wonderful?"

Sophie waved the compliments aside, but she looked pleased all the same.

"She is rather great, isn't she," she said. "Victor says that her propeller will be perfect for giving her the boost she needs. He even thinks she might be able to do aeronautics – you know, loop-the-loop."

Alice frowned. So Victor and Paul were taking an interest in Sophie's plane as well as in Monsieur Alain. Claude had said that their story about being students had been checked, but still, she did not like it.

"Victor is a student, isn't he? I think I saw him in the fashion hall today," Alice said. "He was with his friend, Paul. They came to one of the shows."

Sophie looked quizzical. "How odd," she said. "Though I suppose that's where we met. I was looking for that wadding. Oh, of course! Maybe they were looking for new materials. Materials science is vital for aeronautics, you know. Anything strong and light is useful. If we could only harness the power of spiders' webs, we'd be able to do anything."

"Spiders' webs?" asked Alice.

Sophie nodded. "Incredibly light, incredibly strong. There is a tree down by the river – I don't know what species of spider lives in it, but it is just *covered* in webbing. When it rains it looks like a sparkling jewel with all the water droplets on it. I sometimes take some of the web – just a little, from the lower branches – for study. It's fascinating stuff. Really strong but so light."

Alice stared at her. Sophie thought about things in such incredible detail. It must be why Ariadne was such an impressive feat of engineering. And

her talk with Sophie had confirmed one thing –
Paul and Victor had a good reason for being at
the fashion show. So were they there as innocent
plane enthusiasts, or was there some other reason?
Something more dangerous?

CHAPTER
TWELVE

The next day, after making very sure that Casper had not crept into the taxi behind her, Alice set off for the Fashion pavilion. Madame Éclair had given her a much needed day off and she had worked all day on a new creation that she was eager to unbox in front of the models at the evening's show. She needed to get their attention so that they might tell her more about all the people who visited the shows on a regular basis and this might just do it.

"What on *earth*!" Delphine cried as Alice untied the pink ribbons that held the box shut. The sides fell away, revealing a cake on the top of which was a perfect recreation of the fashion hall. Tiny purple flowers cascaded down the sides. The columns that ran round the room were etched out in ivory icing, and in the centre was a stage on which stood perfectly recreated models of Eva, Delphine and the other models wearing the dresses that they had worn the day before.

"That's *Joie du Printemps*!" Eva said. "Oh, Alice, it's beautiful."

"Wait till you see this," Alice said. She pressed a button on the base of the cake stand and the stage began to rotate, the tiny sugar models each doing a waltz around one another.

"How!" cried Delphine.

Alice laughed. "I built it round a music box," she said. "The cake is hollowed out in the middle. I'm going to do the lozenges as usual, but I'm going to recreate the show with all of you in it as well. By the end of the show the tiny models will all be wearing the dresses from today's show."

"Will mine have the beading *before* Charles starts picking at it or *after*?" muttered Eva. "He really has a cheek. They're Monsieur Fouray's designs, not his. He's meant to improve the fitting and make sure we look our best in them. He's not meant to mess around with the beading and change the designs." She stared at the tiny sugar Eva still spinning round on her music-box stage. "He's already started on me today, you know. The first thing he said was, 'Mam'selle Castillion, you *must* make sure that your stole this afternoon is wrapped left over right. The beading *must* hang correctly.' I mean, what does it matter? It looks the same however I wear it."

Alice didn't really care about Charles. She wanted to know more about the people who came to watch the shows.

"I suppose Madame Grenouille will be here today," she said. "She seems to be at every show."

Delphine laughed. "Oh, that old dear, yes. I don't think she ever buys anything though. I can't think why Monsieur Fouray keeps letting her have tickets."

"Is there anyone else who is here a lot?" asked Alice.

Eva shot her a curious look. "Well, most of us have followers, if that's what you mean?"

Alice blushed. Of course, as they were so beautiful, it was natural that the models would have young men who wanted to take them out to tea, but she hadn't been thinking of romance.

"I meant more … members of the audience. Is there anyone like Madame Grenouille who comes to lots of shows? I saw a man in the front row the other day…"

"Oh, him!" blurted Eva. "Yes, I've seen him at least three times. A Monsieur Lenoir. He always sits in the front row. I'm convinced he is in love with Delphine."

Delphine pulled a face at the thought. "He's always hanging around. He's very clumsy too. He tore a bit of lace off my gown the other day by standing on the train. Charles is furious. It's the fourth gown with tears or snips or missing beading this week."

Eva looked thoughtful. "I reckon he's up to something. You know that one of Paris's most exclusive jewellers loans us some of their more expensive pieces for the shows? I sometimes wonder if Monsieur Lenoir is trying to work out how to steal one. He always takes so much interest in all the costumes, but he never buys a thing."

Alice stared at her. Just a few months before, she had travelled on the Sapphire Express, France's most glamorous train, and had met an English girl called Penelope who turned out to be as good at tracking down thieves as Alice was at tracking down spies. And now here was Eva, suspecting Monsieur Lenoir of something. It would not be safe for Alice to take Eva into her confidence, but perhaps she could encourage her suspicions, whatever they were.

"Oh, and there's Señor Rubio, of course," continued Eva. "His last show was very daring. One of the models had a dress that was entirely made from gold coins. Another had a great coil of wired velvet that wrapped from her shoulder to her hip.

The papers *love* him, of course, but they're not what I'd call wearable."

"He only comes to the shows to annoy Monsieur Fouray," said Delphine. "And to make sure that none of his clients buy Monsieur Fouray's dresses. Have you noticed how he hangs around afterwards? He's always telling them about what poor quality the clothes are or how they'd look awful in them. Dreadful man."

Alice was not so sure. Was it possible that Señor Rubio had more than professional jealousy on his mind? She wanted to ask more questions, but Eva was swept away to have her hair set and Delphine disappeared to find the make-up girls. Alice sighed and went to her spot by the curtain.

"*Chocolat*, Madame Grenouille?" Alice asked, holding out a tray to the old lady. The show was yet another triumph and the scene that had played out the day before was having its encore. Young women jostled politely and, with as much haste as they could conceal, tried to be first in line for a fitting at Monsieur Fouray's. Madame Grenouille, as usual, made no attempt to secure an order, but chatted animatedly to the models.

"So kind of you, my dear," the old lady said, choosing one of the lozenges that had that day's *Majesté du Jour* recreated in glossy chocolate icing. Today it had been Eva who had worn it. It was a column of cream satin cut to fit Eva like a glove. The whisper-thin straps were diamanté and crossed over her throat to trail down her shoulder blades to her waist. To Eva's surprise, Charles had whipped away the matching stole that he had made such a fuss about the moment before she went on stage. "Change of plan," he had hissed, almost pulling Eva over in his haste to remove it, and picking at the beading as he hurried back to his table. Eva had recovered with admirable aplomb and had stepped out on to the stage to gasps of admiration from the audience.

"Such a pretty gown," Madame Grenouille murmured. "When I was young we could never wear anything so daring, of course. It's a new world."

Not for the first time, a shadow of something sad crossed the woman's face. Alice decided that she could take a chance and ask a direct question.

"Why *do* you come to the show every day?"

Madame Grenouille's eyes remained fixed on the drawing of Eva on the chocolate lozenge. She sighed. Something in Alice clenched and she realised that she had taken a step into something painful.

"Could we sit down, do you think, my dear?" Madame Grenouille asked. She looked tired suddenly, and Alice had that familiar feeling of guilt at prying into people's secrets. It was the worst part of being a spy. Sometimes she felt like she was trampling on the most tender and personal parts of people's lives. The innocent got caught up in her search for the guilty and she never knew what damage she was doing till it was too late. Would she ever manage to get it right? She helped Madame Grenouille to a comfortable-looking chair and sat down with her. Madame Grenouille placed the lozenge on a napkin and wiped a tear away from her eye.

"You have guessed, I suppose, that I am a war widow." She motioned to her clothes, and Alice nodded.

"I lost my sons as well as my dear husband," the old lady continued. "All four of them. Two on one day, in the same battle. It was the darkest day of my life. One of them was engaged, to a girl who looked very much like this model here. Of course, after a time she moved on, found new happiness, and I am glad. She is young and beautiful and deserves to live in love and light, not tied to the past, but..." Madame Grenouille reached out a finger and touched the lozenge. "Sometimes it feels like I lost a daughter too. I miss her dreadfully. So I come here to remind myself of happier times, when my home was full of young people laughing and smiling in beautiful clothes. Oh, the parties we used to have! And there are people to talk to here. That helps. It makes me feel less lonely."

Alice's heart broke for the old lady. There was no doubt in her mind that Madame Grenouille was not the spy she was looking for. At least she could cross her off the suspects list. Monsieur Lenoir would be the person to talk with next, she was sure of it. The man who came to every show but, like Madame Grenouille, never made a purchase. She needed to get a look at that button on his lapel. Claude had confirmed that it was not a Daedalus pin. But he had mentioned that the enemy spy rings had insignia. If she could get a look at the pin she could ask Claude to check up on it. Alice glanced around the room and spotted Monsieur Lenoir in conversation with Eva. He was pointing at something on the stage and as Eva turned, Alice saw a quick glint of light as the man slipped something into his pocket. She gasped as she spotted that it was a tiny pair of scissors. What on earth was he up to?

"I must let you go, my dear," Madame Grenouille said, patting her hand. "I've taken up far too much of your time."

Alice smiled at her, instantly guilty at the feeling of relief that she would not have to find a way to extract herself from their conversation. Madame Grenouille was a good woman, but Alice had a job to do.

"I look forward to talking with you again tomorrow," Alice said, putting stress on the word "tomorrow" so that it turned into a promise. She stood and picked up the tray of chocolates from the table. Then she set off for the other side of the room. It was time to find out what she could about Monsieur Lenoir.

CHAPTER THIRTEEN

Eva's smile was bright as she talked to Monsieur Lenoir. *She really is remarkable*, Alice thought. She had the ability to make you feel like you were the most fascinating person in the world. Delphine was famed as the most beautiful of the models, but Eva was the one everyone was drawn to, and after the show she would be surrounded by admirers.

As Alice drew close she slowed to let herself take a good, long look at Monsieur Lenoir. He was still fiddling with his lapel pin in that strange, nervous way of his, but the curve of his fingers hid the design of the pin. Alice was trying to angle her head to see if she could get a better look when Eva spotted her.

"Alice! Oh, Monsieur Lenoir, you just have to meet Alice. She made the cake that everyone is talking about."

Alice smiled and held out her hand.

"Charmed," the man said. "Such beautiful sugar work. Where were you trained, Mam'selle?"

Alice was a little taken aback and admitted that she had learned in her mother's shop.

"Amazing, isn't she?" Eva said, turning that bright smile full on Alice. "I can't draw a circle round a centime."

"Well, *I* couldn't make people fall in love with everything I wore," Alice said. It was the first thing that came into her head to try to turn attention back to Eva, but it was true. People were very snobby about the models – "Just clothes horses with a pulse," one woman had snipped as Eva walked past during the show. But over the past couple of days Alice had realised that there was a skill to their performance that she would never have. Eva, Delphine and the rest of the models were like dancers, each in a duet with whatever they wore, moving to show off not only the skill of their own limbs but the lines and movements of their dresses. Watching them work, Alice had started to hold herself with more confidence, drawing her shoulders back, trying to walk with her chin lifted a little higher. It made her feel just a little more like them. Then, of course, she would trip over something on the ground and feel very much like herself again. Being elegant was far too much like hard work.

"One moment, please, ladies," Monsieur Lenoir said. He placed his hand on his chest and executed a perfect bow before turning on his heel and walking towards the other side of the room.

"I'm scarpering before he comes back," Eva muttered. "Let Delphine take care of him. Wait here and I'll come out with you."

Alice nodded. She wanted to watch Monsieur Lenoir for a little longer. She had been so keen to turn his attention back to Eva that she had not even glanced at his lapel pin, and with that gallant movement before he bowed, he had covered it with his hand. It might have had "I am the spy" written on it for all the good Alice had been in spotting it!

Monsieur Lenoir had crossed to talk to a lady in a striking purple coat and a hat with long peacock-feather plumes. Alice withdrew to the side of the room and then began to drift towards them, hoping that she might eavesdrop. She had almost reached them when she saw Monsieur Lenoir pass something into the woman's hand that was quickly slipped into the pocket of her coat. Then the woman gave a curt nod, strode across the room and left. Alice made up her mind. She *must* follow her. Monsieur Lenoir had handed something over and she wanted to know what. There was no time to wait for Eva. She dashed to the door.

The woman had turned right, Alice was sure of

it, towards the walkway that led to the Ceramics pavilion. Alice wove her way through the crowds, trying to catch sight of the peacock plume. A presentation in one of the nearby rooms finished and a tide of visitors poured into the hallway and bore down on her, eager to get to the next delight that the fair had to offer. Alice was buffeted on all sides as the crowd crossed over itself, milling around the increasingly small space, cramming her against walls and tripping her up. As Alice rounded a corner at the end of the walkway she spotted the green-blue eye of the peacock feather whisk towards the stairs. She pushed on through the crowd down to the next level and fought her way through to the doors of the pavilion, where the masses of people spilled out on to the street. The woman was turning towards the end of the road where a line of taxis stood waiting for fares. Alice's hand went to her pocket, but it was pointless. Her purse was in her handbag, tucked safely away backstage in the hall. She watched in dismay as the woman got into a taxi and closed the door.

Alice let out a groan of frustration and kicked at the ground. She had blown it. She was about to go back into the pavilion when she heard a roar behind her and a motorcycle drew up at the kerb.

"I thought you were going to wait for me," said the motorcyclist, taking off their helmet and shaking out their hair. Alice gasped. It was Eva, dressed very curiously indeed in a thick grey serge jacket and trousers that seemed better suited for winter than a warm summer's evening.

"Well, come on," said Eva. "You look like you've found a penny and lost sixpence. What's so important that you had to dash off like that?"

Alice glanced at the taxi rank. The woman's taxi had not yet moved off.

"Eva, could I borrow some money?" she asked. "I need to follow that taxi. Monsieur Lenoir passed something to the woman in it and I need to find out what."

Eva gasped. "I *told* you he was up to something! No need for a taxi though. Hang on."

Eva swung herself off the motorcycle and dug around in a box at the back. She drew out a bundle and threw it at Alice. Catching it, Alice found that it was a helmet, a thick jacket and pair of overtrousers.

"I always carry spares," said Eva. "Quick, pop them on and jump on."

Alice stared at the bike. Her mother would refuse to let her out of the house for a month if she found out that Alice had even *thought* of riding on the back of a motorbike. But if they were to follow the mystery woman... She pulled the helmet on, tightening the straps snugly under her chin, but paused at the clothes. The evening was very warm and the jacket looked to be made of very thick wool.

"Do I really need these?" she asked.

"Yes!" said Eva in an exasperated tone. "I won't let anyone on the back of my bike without proper clothing. The smallest fall can do a lot of damage. Now, hurry up. Her taxi just pulled out of the line. Get on and hold on tight. I don't want to lose you on any of the corners."

Alice pulled on the jacket and trousers and swung herself on to the back of the cycle. She threw her arms round Eva's waist and took a deep breath. She could feel her heart beating very fast under her ribcage. Alice had climbed along the side of a steam train and jumped from carriage to carriage, but somehow the thought of hurtling through Paris on the back of a motorcycle was utterly terrifying.

Eva kicked a stand at the side of the bike and it leapt forwards. Alice crushed herself against Eva's back and squeezed her eyes tight shut. She felt the air rush against her face, and when she opened her mouth to ask whether they could possibly go a little slower she found the words pushed back into her throat.

Alice felt Eva swing the bike to the right and almost screamed as they leaned alarmingly into the turn.

"Let me do all the work," Eva shouted, her voice thin as it rushed past Alice's ears. "Just keep holding on; you're doing fine. You might want to open your eyes though, so you can tell me which way she goes next. I need to concentrate on the driving."

Alice gave a great swallow and forced herself to open her eyes. Paris sped by on either side of them, the lights of the city blurring against the night. She peered over Eva's shoulder and saw the taxi with the mystery woman take a right-hand turn at the end of one of the bridges and head off towards the east of the city.

"Right!" Alice shouted in Eva's ear. She felt Eva

nod and swerve the cycle into the right-hand lane. They swung round on to the road leading away from the city centre, the bike picking up speed, the air around them melting away as they cut through it. It was almost the same feeling as flying above the city with Sophie the night before. As the taxi took a left turn, Alice shouted at Eva again and they sped off into the night.

About half an hour later, when Alice thought that her arms would drop off from clinging on to Eva so tight, they saw the taxicab turn down a side street and slow to a stop. Eva carried on past the turning for a few metres, then drew up by the kerb and looked back at Alice.

"Come on," she hissed. "Let's see what she's up to."

Alice tipped herself off the back of the seat. Everything seemed to be aching and she could hardly feel the blood in her hands from having clutched so tightly at Eva's coat. They moved as quietly as possible down the street and slipped into the shadows at the end, out of sight of the taxi.

"Can you hear that?" Eva whispered.

Alice nodded. The air was thrumming with the

sound of machinery, a steady rhythm of something that clattered like a typewriter.

"Could it be a printing press?" Alice asked.

Eva shrugged.

The woman hurried up a flight of stairs at the end of the building and let herself in through a metal door. Alice and Eva shrank back further into the shadows till she had closed the door behind her.

"Go, now!" hissed Eva, elbowing Alice in the ribs. They edged out of the alleyway, ran a little way down the street and slipped behind a post box, watching as the taxicab pulled out of the street and turned back towards the centre of the city. Then Alice stepped out and led the way back towards the building. Monsieur Lenoir had passed something to the woman inside, and she was determined to find out what.

CHAPTER
FOURTEEN

Alice crept along the side of the building with Eva close behind her. About halfway down the alleyway she realised how ridiculous it was that they were trying to be quiet, when the air was throbbing with the sound of the machinery within. She looked up at the windows high above them and wondered how they could get a glimpse of what was going on inside.

"I don't think we should go up the steps," she said to Eva. "I'm going to shin up that drainpipe and look in the window." She pointed to the end of the building near the steps the woman had come down, and Eva nodded.

"Well, in that case, I'm going up one too," she said, and before Alice could stop her she had grabbed hold of the pipe nearest to them and was halfway up the wall. She must have heard Alice's little gasp of surprise because she turned and pulled a face at her.

"I'm not *just* pretty dresses and smiles, you know," she said with a smile.

Alice grinned at her and dashed to the end of the building. The sound of the machines was more muffled here. She glanced over at Eva, who had reached the windows and was peering in.

"Anything?" she hissed at her.

Eva nodded and began to clamber down to the ground. Alice took hold of the drainpipe and started to climb towards the window above her. She had just reached eye level with the room when Eva appeared below her.

"They're making clothes," Eva whispered. "Hundreds of women at sewing machines, and you'll never guess what the strangest thing is—"

"Shhh," hissed Alice, peering in through the window. She was looking into an office of sorts. The walls were papered with drawings of elegant gowns, and rolls of fabric were stacked up in the corner. Along one wall was a desk with a drawing easel on top and pencil pots stuffed full of pens and brushes.

Alice stared at the pictures on the wall. Every one of them was an image of the dresses she had been drawing at the fashion show. There was the chiffon creation that Eva had worn on the first day, and the hand-painted dress that Delphine had looked so beautiful in. As she stared, a door opened and the woman she had seen in the alleyway entered the office, clicking off a red light in the room next door.

"A darkroom," hissed Alice at Eva, as she ducked her head out of sight. "Monsieur Lenoir must have passed her a film!"

"What!" hissed Eva. "I'm not missing this!" and to Alice's horror she dashed up the steps and peered through the window in the door.

Alice peered back over the windowsill and watched the woman walk to the easel and pin a roll of film to a white box that stood next to it. The woman pressed a button and the box lit up, shining through the film. The woman picked up a monocle spyglass, put it to her eye and, peering closely at the film, began to draw out lines of dresses on a piece of paper on the easel.

Alice stared in surprise as the woman sketched out the lines of the dress that Eva had worn at the show that evening. She glanced down at Eva, but her friend was wearing an expression that told Alice she knew *exactly* what was going on.

"Alice, look!" Eva hissed. "It was more than a film he passed to her. Look at the board! I think we know where all those scraps of fabric and beads went. The CHEEK of the man!"

Alice looked again. The woman was pinning

scraps of fabric and lace to a cork board in front of her, making notes about them on her drawing. Eva was right. Monsieur Lenoir must have been tearing and snipping pieces of fabric from the dresses all the time and passing them along with his photos to this woman. But why?

Alice shinned down a little way and then dropped to the ground.

Eva dashed down the steps to meet her. She looked furious. "The minute I saw what they were sewing in the main room, I knew. They are making cheap copies of Monsieur Fouray's designs. It's a problem for all the big fashion houses. They'll flood the shops with them by morning, before the papers even have time to print their photos from the shows."

"So Monsieur Lenoir *is* a spy," muttered Alice.

"It looks like it," said Eva. "I wonder how he took the photos though. I never saw him with a camera."

Alice thought for a moment. "I did!" she cried. "Well, not a camera, but a lens. You know he is always fiddling with that button on his lapel? I thought it must be some sort of nervous habit, but I think *that's* where he keeps his camera. He must have been taking photographs of every show. We have to tell Monsieur Fouray as soon as possible."

Eva nodded. "First thing tomorrow. I suspect he'll have great fun letting Monsieur Lenoir know he is no longer welcome at the shows. Urgh, that man! I could spit! Monsieur Fouray takes all that time making the most beautiful clothes and that … that *leech* just steals the designs and makes them overnight before Monsieur Fouray has a chance."

Alice smiled. Eva really was very loyal, and it *was* awful that Monsieur Fouray's work was being stolen. So Monsieur Lenoir had turned out to be a spy after all, just not the sort that Alice thought he was. She remembered Uncle Robert telling her about Industrial Espionage, when companies stole each other's secrets. He had been very sniffy about it. "I never got involved in that," he had told Alice. "Some things are beneath a spy."

Something else you were wrong about, Uncle Robert, thought Alice. *And I was wrong too. When it comes to being loyal to friends and protecting their hard work, nothing is beneath the interest of a good spy.*

They rode back to the centre of the city rather more slowly. Eva was all for roaring through the traffic, but Alice begged her to take a more sedate pace. She found the whole experience terrifying and even at a much slower speed she clung so tight to Eva's waist that her knuckles turned white. As they reached the banks of the Seine, the clocks began to chime nine o'clock and Alice heard the sound of the nightly firework displays that the city was putting on to entertain its visitors. They pulled over to the side of the road and watched as the night sky turned into a jewellery box of glittering diamond starbursts and streams of emerald and sapphire. Alice thought for one moment that it would be so lovely to be able to enjoy the fair as a visitor without worrying about stolen aircraft plans or kidnapped spies, or even Monsieur Lenoir and his appalling thievery. But it was only a fleeting thought. As a rocket climbed high into the sky to explode above the Eiffel Tower, showering the river in sparkling light, Alice was already trying to puzzle something out. If Monsieur Lenoir was not the spy she was looking for, then who was?

CHAPTER
FIFTEEN

The next morning, as soon as she had helped Madame Éclair set up their stall in the Tastes of the World pavilion, Alice made a beeline for the fashion hall, where Eva was already deep in conversation with Monsieur Fouray.

"I've told him everything," Eva said, looking up as Alice entered the room. "Monsieur Lenoir won't be welcome at any more shows."

"We know these things happen, obviously," Monsieur Fouray said. "But I thought that we had been so careful. We only allow press photographers, carefully screened and interviewed. We guard the designs so carefully, even from you, Mam'selle."

Alice nodded. In that moment she realised that, had she not helped unmask Monsieur Lenoir, Alice herself might have been suspected of being the spy. After all, she had proved herself expert at drawing the dress designs. How easy it would have been for her to fall under suspicion.

"We don't have any shows today, Mam'selle," Monsieur Fouray said, "but I have a very special commission for you, and after seeing your incredible work yesterday I am sure it will not be too large a request."

Monsieur Fouray looked even more stressed than usual. His hair stuck up at odd angles as though he had run his hand through it one too many times, and his usually neat tie was askew.

"The truth is, Mam'selle," he said. "That imposter Rubio will not leave me alone. I know he has something planned. Something that he will call a spectacular. Pah! An affront to taste, that is what his spectaculars are, but do the papers care? No! They will print him all over their front pages anyway. But we can foil his plan."

He ushered Alice towards an easel in the middle of the room and, after glancing round to check that no one had entered the room behind them, flipped the sheet of paper over. Alice gasped.

"Can you do it, do you think, Mam'selle? Say you can. You can, I know it."

Alice thought quickly. The fact that Monsieur Fouray was even showing her this was proof that he trusted her. She badly wanted to repay that trust, but the construction of what he wanted … she was not sure that even the most skilled sugarsmith in France would be able to achieve it. But if she said no? She could not risk losing her place backstage at the fashion shows. Not till she knew who the spy was.

"Wouldn't it be wonderful," breathed Eva.

Alice nodded. "I can do it," she said. "I'll bring it over tomorrow afternoon, before the show."

She left the Fashion pavilion, her mind buzzing. How on earth was she going to manage this? She wandered through the fair, planning out possibilities in her mind, but although she had promised Monsieur Fouray that she *could* do it, she did not know *how*.

By the time she reached the Palais de l'Air, she was convinced that she would be falling flat on her face the next day, with nothing to show Monsieur Fouray and Eva. She walked into the great aerodrome and looked up at the balloon suspended from the roof, its canopy billowing out as though filled ready for flight. She was peering at the wires that held it high aloft when she heard Sophie's voice. Her friend was walking across one of the walkways above, chatting to two young men. Alice tensed. It was Victor and Paul, the students she had seen a few days earlier.

"It's only a small craft, but I'm really proud of it," Sophie was saying. She was clearly talking about the plane she had invented.

"Don't tell them anything, Sophie," Alice muttered under her breath. Why were they always hanging around the pavilion, talking with Sophie and her father? Why were they so keen to investigate new materials? Claude had said that their stories had been checked. But Alice was still full of doubts.

She remembered that discussion with Claude after the mission on the boat. What was it he had said? That her gut could always be trusted. And Alice's gut was telling her that these men spelled danger.

She dashed to the steps that led to the upper walkways and, taking them two at a time, ran to catch up with Sophie and the two men. She was quite out of breath by the time she reached them. They were discussing the rope patterns on the balloon and the heights it could reach before its passengers needed to release some of the gas in it and descend.

"Such an old-fashioned way of travelling though," Victor was saying. "Why be held back by something from the eighteenth century? We should look to the future."

"Like you are doing, Sophie," offered Paul. "I'm really looking forward to seeing this new plane of yours."

"Well, it's meant to be a surprise, really," started Sophie. Then, spotting Alice, she waved her over. Did Alice imagine it, or did Victor look annoyed when he saw her?

"Victor and Paul want to meet Ariadne," she said. "I know she's meant to be a surprise, but they've promised not to tell anyone about her."

Alice frowned. "Are you sure?" she asked. "I mean, won't it spoil the surprise if too many people see her before you make your flight?"

Sophie looked as though she was thinking about this, but Victor stepped forward and placed himself between Sophie and Alice.

"Nonsense," he said, laughing with a smile that did not reach his eyes. "Paul and I will be sworn to secrecy, won't we. You can absolutely trust us."

"I suppose it *will* be all right," said Sophie. Alice tried to lean round to catch her eye, but Victor was in the way and Paul grabbed at Sophie's elbow and pulled her towards the ladder that led to the roof.

"You said it was this way," he cried, pushing on

ahead. "No time like the present."

They clambered up the ladder and through the hatch to the roof. Paul was out first, then Sophie, and Victor followed in front of Alice. At the top he let the hatch fall back into place, slamming smartly on Alice's knuckles so that she cried out with pain and nearly let go of the ladder. Her head swam as she looked down into the great cavern of the aerodrome. The hatch flew open and Sophie's face appeared, pink with anger.

"Are you OK, Alice?" her friend asked, reaching out a hand to help her up on to the roof. She looked back at Victor and Paul.

"You *never* let go of the hatch till everyone is safely through," she snapped. "I had to work hard to persuade Papa to let me build up here and he is *very* strict on safety."

"I'm fine, honest," said Alice, rubbing at the bruise that was rising on her hand. She flexed the fingers a few times and hoped that they would not be too sore for all the fine decorating work that Monsieur Fouray needed from her.

"It was only a little bump," Paul said, pulling Sophie away from Alice.

"So this is Ariadne," Victor said. He pulled a notebook out of his pocket and began to scribble. Alice saw a look of concern cross Sophie's face.

"I'd rather you didn't," she said. "It's meant to be a secret."

Victor waved her aside. "I'm just sketching. I love to make drawings of aeroplanes. Don't I, Paul?"

Alice bristled. Sophie did not want them sketching her plane, and neither did she. She was more sure than ever that these men were up to something. Sophie was too polite to stop them, but Alice knew she had to act.

"Let me see," she said, pushing past Paul and glancing over Victor's shoulder. He snapped the notebook shut and glared at her.

"Maybe Sophie is right," he huffed. "I can make a drawing of it when she is in the air."

Just as I suspected, thought Alice. *He wasn't drawing. He was making notes of some kind.* Victor tried to move away to the side, but Alice stuck to him like glue. She wasn't going to give him another chance to open that notebook of his.

"It's an amazing piece of work," Paul said, walking round the plane, examining the wings. "How long did it take you to build?"

"Not as long as I thought it would," Sophie said. "And we were lucky. We were the first people in the Palais. We've been here weeks before it opened, so I've had time to carry pieces up here and build."

"And she's your own design?" Victor asked.

Sophie nodded. "Papa taught me all about planes from when I was tiny. I've always wanted to build my own, and when Papa told me that the next great breakthrough was to be in gliding further without power – well, I just *had* to see if I could solve it."

Alice saw Victor raise one eyebrow at Paul. There was a warning in it and Alice felt a prickle of fear. They were up to something and it was linked to Sophie's plane. What was it she had said about Ariadne? That she could glide further than any plane of her size. The Daedalus was meant to be able to travel further than any other plane. Could they possibly be linked? Surely not, but then, why were Paul and Victor so interested? Monsieur Alain's plane was much bigger than Sophie's little glider.

"It's amazing, Sophie," Paul said. "I can't wait to see you fly it tomorrow night."

"As long as I can make it to the Chaillot Palace,

I won't have disgraced myself," said Sophie.

Victor laughed. "You could fly to the sun and back in this, I'm sure," he said, and Alice saw Paul smirk. It was not a nice look. There was something going on between them, some conversation that Sophie and Alice were not a part of.

Claude was wrong about them, she thought. He may have dismissed them as innocent students, but she was not convinced. These two were up to something, and it was down to her to work out what.

CHAPTER SIXTEEN

Alice spent the next morning in *Vive Comme L'Éclair*, spinning sugar to create the masterpieces that Monsieur Fouray had requested. It was hot work and the first three batches had been discarded as Alice struggled to get them to just the consistency that she needed.

"I don't have *time* for this," she groaned, throwing her wooden spoon into yet another burned mess and shooting a look at the clock. It was almost eleven o'clock and she needed to be at the afternoon show. And goodness knows what Paul and Victor had been up to while she was spinning sugar and shooing Casper out of the kitchen. She had been tempted to give up and tell Monsieur Fouray that what he had asked for was impossible, but then she might lose her place at the show and that was unthinkable.

Casper wound himself round her feet and miaowed for treats.

"How on earth can you think about your stomach at a time like this?" she scolded. "You can go back out the front. We don't have mice, so you are not needed here."

"Casper is not a cat who can be reasoned with,"

said Madame Éclair, walking into the kitchen with a bag full of deliveries from Minou's, the finest confectioner in Paris. She clicked her fingers at the white cat and said one stern word.

"Out!"

Casper miaowed in complaint and slunk out of the door.

Madame Éclair put the bag on the kitchen table and glanced at the saucepans soaking in the sink. Each one of them had burned sugar welded to the bottom. She looked at Alice and frowned.

"I'm sure Monsieur Fouray would not mind if you presented something else today, Alice," she said. "I shouldn't say this, perhaps, but after all it is only cake." She took Alice's face in her hands. "You don't look happy and, my darling girl, you are more important than cake. It's not worth you getting so upset and stressed."

Alice sighed. Not for the first time, she wished she could take Madame Éclair into her confidence, but she did not want to worry her mother, and she knew that if Madame Éclair knew how much danger she was in, she would put a stop to it at once. Alice gave her mother a quick kiss on the cheek.

"I'll be fine, *Maman*," she said. "I'll give it one last go. It will be easier without Casper under my feet."

After Madame Éclair had returned to the shop, Alice blew away a stray hair that had stuck to her warm brow, took a deep breath and started again. Whisking a spoonful of caramel out of the pan, she watched as it glimmered in the light. She drew her hand far above her shoulder till the sugar spun itself into a strand as fine as spider's silk, then she picked up an icing-coated balloon inflated to the size of her palm. Alice whipped the sugar round the balloon, layer upon layer till it was a filigree cage. She waited a few seconds, then picked up a long pin and popped the balloon, laying the sugar orb down on the counter.

She worked across the trays till thirty glistening sugar cages sat on the counter before her. Alice breathed a sigh of relief. Maybe, just maybe, she could do this after all.

It was two o'clock when Alice was ready to leave the shop. She had parcelled her work carefully into boxes lined with crumpled baking parchment. Each precious orb was wrapped in rice paper and laid in a tray that a few days before had held delicate peaches delivered by Paris's most exclusive fruit merchant. The slightest knock could ruin her hard work. Stepping carefully over Casper, who was washing his paws and hoping for a spare morsel of cream, she set off to find a taxi. Casper miaowed in annoyance as she left.

The taxi sped across the city and Alice looked out at the crowds enjoying walks by the Seine or admiring the flower displays hung from the Eiffel Tower. As they pulled on to the main road that ran alongside the Seine, they were overtaken by a motorcyclist with a mass of glossy dark curls peeking out from under their helmet. It was Eva.

Alice asked the taxi to pull up as close to the Fashion pavilion as they could, and carried the boxes through the great doors, nodding her thanks to the steward who kindly held them for her. "Another masterpiece, Miss Éclair?" he smiled at her. "You are becoming quite famous, you know. All the ladies from Monsieur Fouray's shows are talking about you."

Alice smiled, but in that instant she felt her foot trip over something. She glanced down to see

Casper, miaowing at her in annoyance. Her leg went from under her and she felt the boxes in her hands tilt. She cried out, willed herself to not let go. There was nothing she could do to stop herself from falling towards the hard floor, feeling the precious creations in her boxes bounce around, knowing that the delicate sugar would be cracking, falling away to nothing but crumbs.

And in a flash she was back on the motorcycle with Eva, dashing through the city, clinging to her friend's waist as they rounded corners, Eva leaning into the tip of the vehicle and yelling at Alice not to fight against it.

Don't fight it, she told herself.

She kept the boxes balanced and allowed her leg to slip away in front of her. She leaned over to keep the boxes upright, and her other leg fell behind, arching away till Alice found herself executing a perfect pair of splits in the middle of the floor, the boxes tied with the distinctive sea-green ribbon of the *Vive Comme L'Éclair* held high above her head.

"Miss Éclair!" the steward cried in alarm. He dashed to help her up, but Alice thrust the boxes at him and clambered to her feet herself. At least they had not hit the floor. Perhaps something inside could be salvaged.

She turned on Casper.

"What on earth are you doing here?" she demanded. "I suppose you followed me into the taxi. Ridiculous animal!" In response, Casper licked his paw. Alice groaned. "Well, you'd better stay with me now," she retorted.

And with that, Alice brushed herself down, retrieved her boxes and set off into the pavilion for the fashion show.

The backstage area was abuzz. The hair stylist dashed past her, her own hair escaping from its tight chignon and cascading in messy strands down her shoulders. One of the make-up girls was face-deep in her bag muttering frantically about eyelash curlers. Alice looked around for Eva. She was being fitted into a column of white satin by a girl with a row of pins in her mouth. A mass of gold seed beads cascaded down the front of the dress and ran round the hem, interspersed with longer bugle beads. As usual, Eva looked magnificent, her dark hair pinned into glossy coils on top of her head.

"Mam'selle Éclair!"

It was Monsieur Fouray, the only person there who seemed not to be in a total panic. He took one look at the boxes in Alice's hands and let out a sigh.

"I *knew* you could do it," he said. "You must let me see."

He pushed aside a pile of clothes that were set on a table nearby and motioned for Alice to set down the boxes. She undid the ribbon of the top one and let the sides fall away, holding her breath to see how much damage her fall had done.

Monsieur Fouray let out a low whistle.

"*Exquisite.*"

Nestled in the peach trays were the filigree orbs of spun sugar. Inside each orb hung a tiny dress, suspended from its caramel cage by the thinnest of sugar strands. Each dress was different, a perfect replica of one of the dresses from Monsieur Fouray's shows.

The honeysuckle blooms from the dress Delphine had worn were picked out in delicate pink sugar. Eva's silver gown was spun out of transparent sugar with a glycerine wash so that it shimmered in the light. Alice was relieved to see that they had come to no harm. She felt in her pocket, where she had secreted three full icing cones, just in case they were needed for what her mother called "running repairs". They would not be needed after all, and she hoped that they did not melt in the summer heat and ruin her jacket.

"Perfect, Mam'selle. I think even Charles will be content with these," said Monsieur Fouray. He glanced around for his assistant, but Charles was busy with one of the models, showing her the perfect way to move her dress to show off the hand-painted flowers that flowed down one side of the bodice. He was just modelling how to sweep her arm up when one of the pavilion staff, whose job it was to run around passing messages, took him aside and passed him a note. Charles waved them away and, scrunching the note into his pocket, made straight for the exit, leaving the messenger staring after him.

Alice nodded to Monsieur Fouray and covered the orbs with the box lid to keep them safe until after the show. Then she made her way over to the messenger, who was checking something in a slim notebook.

"Where has Monsieur Deforges gone?" Alice asked, trying to keep her voice light, in spite of being *desperately* curious. The girl looked up and shrugged. "There was a message for him on the telephone at the pavilion entrance," she said.

Alice raised an eyebrow. The halls did not have their own phones, but urgent messages could be passed through the pavilion telephones and relayed by messengers. She was used to the liveried young people dashing through with well wishes for the models or with requests for orders for Monsieur Fouray, but whoever had phoned Charles had not wanted to leave a message. Could it be because whatever they had to say was for Charles's ears only?

It was almost time for the show to begin by the time that Charles returned, red faced and flustered. Monsieur Fouray had gone out to greet the audience, who were gathering around the tables in the fashion hall, and the models were lining up, ready for their first entrance. Alice heard Monsieur Fouray introduce Eva, and the curtain was drawn back for her to step out on to the stage when Charles grabbed her arm and pulled her back.

"Not you," he snapped. "Delphine, you go out first."

Delphine looked confused. "But Monsieur Fouray has introduced Eva. They will be expecting to see *Evening Jasmine*."

Charles's face grew dark and he shoved Delphine hard in the small of her back.

"I said get on stage, *now*," he hissed, pushing her through the curtain.

As the other models whispered in shocked tones to one another, Charles dropped to his knees and began to snip at the beads from Eva's dress. Then he whisked out a needle from a silver case he carried in a pocket and stitched them back on, closer to the hem. Alice caught Eva's eye and raised an eyebrow in question, but Eva only shrugged. Charles had been very picky about the dress designs before, but he had never behaved this badly. From the auditorium, Alice heard Monsieur Fouray's voice falter, before he slipped smoothly back into the charming tones that they were so used to.

"A thousand pardons, ladies and gentlemen," he said. "Before we see *Evening Jasmine*, we will see Delphine modelling *Moonlight Crystal* for you."

Charles pushed Eva back into line and she tweaked back the curtain so that she could catch Monsieur Fouray's eye and let him know that she was now ready for her entrance. Alice saw her face redden with embarrassment. This would all look like it was Eva's fault, and she was sure that Charles would try to blame her in some way. There was something very odd about the way that he was behaving and as her friend stepped out to show off *Evening Jasmine* to sighs and applause from the audience, Alice decided that she would have to have a good look at the beading on that dress.

CHAPTER SEVENTEEN

Alice waited until Eva had done her sweep of the room, gathering compliments and admiring glances in the train of her dress. As Eva stepped through the curtains into the backstage area, breathing a sigh of relief, Alice hurried forwards and offered to help her change into her next gown.

"Oh, *would* you?" Eva said gratefully. "I'd ask Marie, but she'll be busy getting Delphine into her next one. It's got loads of chiffon to arrange, so I don't think she'll have time for me too. My next one is much simpler."

The "much simpler" gown turned out to be an exquisitely cut dress in hand-painted pink silk with a wide sash that draped in a concertina down the side. As soon as Alice had helped Eva into it, she lifted *Evening Jasmine* from the chair where Eva had laid it and draped it across her arms.

"I'll go and hang this up," she said, and left Eva touching up her lipstick.

Alice walked as slowly as she could towards the dress rail, staring at the beading of the dress. She knew that it had reminded her of something, with its small round seed beads and the long bugle beads. It looked like Morse code, but how could something that swirled as much as this beading did be read as code? She hung the dress on the rail and dropped to her knees to trace a line of beads with her finger from the rosette at the dress's waist down to the hem.

Five seed beads then a gap, then a seed bead and four bugle beads. If these were the dots and dashes of Morse, then this was the number fifty-one.

Alice glanced around, then carried on along the line.

Dot dash dot. Dot dot dash. Dash dot dot.

RUE

Alice gasped. She was right. It was an address. She carried on.

"Fifty-one Rue de Marque. Mme Bouillard. Two. Three extras. Children. Four o'clock."

Alice's head reeled. All this time, Charles had been passing on information using the beading in the dresses. That was why he insisted that they pause for so long as they walked round the room – to give whoever it was time to read the code, or maybe to take a photograph. Alice wondered whether Monsieur Fouray had been as careful as he thought at choosing the press photographers.

As Alice stood up, she realised that, as Eva had worn this dress, then the address of whoever lived at Rue de Marque was known to whoever this had been a signal to. Were they in danger? She must warn Claude at once. She glanced at her wristwatch and, with dismay, realised that it was already three fifteen. Rue de Marque was on the other side of the city. There was no time. Unless… She spun on her heel and ran across the crowded room.

"Eva," whispered Alice. "How many more dresses do you have to show? Are you doing the *Majesté du Jour*?"

Eva was about to go on stage. Without taking her eyes off the curtain, waiting for her entrance, she shook her head. "Delphine is doing today's. I'm very envious. It's supposed to be gorgeous. I've just got this to show and then I can put my feet up."

"I need to borrow you. I can't tell you why but it's an emergency."

At this, Eva flicked a sideways glance towards Alice. "And I suppose this involves Celeste in some way."

"Celeste?"

"One should always name one's motor bicycle,"

Eva said in a faux posh voice, smiling. "It makes them run better."

"Oh. Well, yes, it does involve Celeste. I wouldn't ask if it wasn't really important."

"I'll walk extra quick," promised Eva. "Charles won't like it, but then I don't like him. Meet me back here." And she stepped through the curtain to gasps from the audience.

Ten minutes later they were speeding away from the Fashion pavilion on the back of Eva's motorcycle. Alice was grateful that Eva had not asked any questions. She did not like lying to friends and over the short space of time that they had known each other, Eva had become a friend.

As they turned on to Rue de Marque, Alice felt her heart beating hard in her chest. What if the enemy spies had already reached the family? What might she find in the house? They drew up outside a small house with neatly kept window boxes. A fluffy grey cat peered out from behind the curtains of a window on the ground floor.

Alice clambered off the motorcycle and warned Eva to wait around the corner. She did not want to put her friend in any danger. Eva looked at her quizzically, but pulled away and soon she had disappeared around the end of the street, leaving Alice on the doorstep.

Alice reached up to the gilt knocker on the door and gave it one loud rap. There was an agonising wait and she scanned the street behind her to watch for anyone else arriving, but eventually the door opened a crack and a woman wearing a navy dress and a flour-covered pinafore looked Alice up and down.

"Madame Bouillard?" Alice whispered.

The woman drew back a step, wary. Alice realised that she could be putting herself in great danger. She was about to reveal herself as a spy for France, and if she was wrong about Madame Bouillard being one of their agents… If the woman was one of the enemy instead…

On the other hand, if she did not reveal who she was, she could not hope to get Madame Bouillard to trust her. She stepped forward so that her foot was between the door and the frame, in case the woman tried to close it.

"Madame Bouillard, I am a friend, please trust

me. I know who you are and I know that you and your family are in danger. There are people coming for you, any minute. I need to get you to somewhere safe."

The woman blinked at her and then whipped the door back and slammed it shut with all her strength. Instinctively, Alice snatched her foot out of the way before her toes were crushed.

"Well, *that* went well," she muttered to herself, staring at the blue front door.

Alice racked her brain. There must be *something* she could do to get the woman to trust her. From inside the house she heard frantic movements. The family must think that she was there to harm them. There were raised voices and then agonised shushings. Alice ran a hand distractedly across the back of her neck. And she felt her palm graze on the button pin that Claude had given her, the calling card for anyone who knew about the Daedalus plans. She unpinned it and looked down at the small wing in her palm.

She needed to get into this house. Might this be the key?

Well, I have nothing else to lose, Alice thought.

She ran her hand under the base of the door, found a gap and slipped the pin through. Then she hammered noisily on the door. There were footsteps inside the house. She heard them clatter against the tiles in the hall, saw a shadow move past the frosted glass and pause.

Then the door opened a crack. The woman stood there with the pin in her hand.

"Who sent you?" she asked.

Alice quickly told her all that she knew. Madame Bouillard eyed her warily but eventually she opened the door enough for Alice to step over the threshold.

"You had better have this back," Madame Bouillard said, handing over the pin. "We must leave at once. I knew this day would come. Do you have a safe house for us?"

Alice felt her heart sink. She had not planned for this. She had only thought of warning them. But of course they would need somewhere safe to hide and she had nowhere to offer them.

"Not yet. I know somewhere we can go while we find one," she said. "But I came here on a motorcycle."

Madame Bouillard waved aside her objection. "We have a car. Go now. We will follow."

A small child of about four came clattering down the stairs, followed by an older girl, dragging a suitcase and a cat basket.

Madame Bouillard ran a hand across her brow.

"Marie, there may not be space…"

"Albie's coming too!" growled the child, and she dashed into the room where Alice had seen the small grey cat, almost colliding with a tall man carrying a toddler.

"We're at the far end of the street," Alice said. "We'll wait for you—"

She was interrupted by a hammering on the front door. Madame Bouillard froze.

"Out the back, now!" hissed Monsieur Bouillard. Madame Bouillard grabbed the small boy's hand and dragged him down the hallway towards the back of the house. Her husband followed with the other two children. Alice grabbed hold of the cat basket from the girl so that she could take her father's hand.

The hammering on the front door grew louder. There were shouts and the sound of something being wedged into the door frame.

Madame Bouillard hurried them all out through a small kitchen at the back of the house and into a yard. They dashed across, dodging under a washing line full of towels and nappies, and wrenched open the gate. As they fled into the street behind, they heard breaking glass as the front door of the house splintered open.

They were running now, the children almost pulled off their feet as the frightened parents raced for the small car that stood at the end of the street. Alice felt her chest burning, with fear as much as with the effort. Madame Bouillard reached the car first and flustered for her keys, her hands shaking as she struggled with the lock. Monsieur Bouillard and Alice caught up soon after and threw the children into the back seat, together with Albie's cat basket.

"Go, go quickly," Alice hissed, and she set off down the street at full pelt to meet Eva, hearing the car rev behind her. As she reached the end of the road she glanced round the corner. Eva was waiting, parked on the kerb with the engine running.

"We need to head into the city, as fast as we can," she said, clambering on board. "There is a car behind us that we cannot lose and there may soon be another that we *need* to lose."

Eva let out a low whistle.

"Whatever you are involved with," she said, "I've a feeling it's more exciting than dressing up in frocks for a living."

They rocketed through the city so fast that Alice thought that she would not be able to draw a breath. She kept glancing behind to check that the

Bouillards' car was keeping up with them. At one point she spotted another vehicle following close on their tail. Alice yelled a warning into Eva's ear and the girl nodded and took a sudden swerve to the left. The Bouillards followed and they headed down a narrow alley. At the end, Eva swerved right and they joined a stream of traffic heading towards one of the city bridges. Alice checked behind. The Bouillards were still close behind them. They had gained a little time over the other car, but it was still in sight. Eva swung on to the bridge. It was crowded with traffic, the cars weaving between one another.

"We're slowing!" Eva groaned.

Alice's mind raced. Ahead of them at the end of the bridge a family ushered their five children through the traffic.

"It must be one of the river displays!" Alice yelled. "Drive back towards their car. The traffic on the bridge will slow as people cross to watch the floats pass underneath."

Eva nodded and began to weave her way down the bridge, dodging the cars that were coming towards them. As they passed the Bouillards' car, Alice registered the fear on the face of Madame

Bouillard. Eva waved an arm at them, motioning them to carry on driving forwards for as long as they could. The rest of the traffic was slowing to a crawl. Eva pressed on the accelerator and headed straight towards the car that had been following them. Alice felt her heart beating wildly. Then, gripping the side of the bike with her knees and hoping that she would be able to keep her balance, she grabbed the icing cones from her pocket and ripped them open. The traffic had stopped now. Some drivers had even got out of their vehicles to look down at the spectacular display below. As they neared the car, Alice could see the men inside shouting angrily at the cars in front of them, honking the horn and waving their hands to urge the traffic to start up again, but it was no use. Alice had seen this the first day of the fair as they'd tried to get home, tired heads buzzing with the fuss of the first day. Everything stopped for the fair's wonderful river displays. Her hand tightened on the icing cones. As they passed by the car, she took aim and scored a direct hit with all three in the centre of the car's windscreen. The cones exploded, leaving the glass coated with glossy royal icing. It ran in rivulets down the screen and Alice heard the driver inside let out a roar of anger.

Eva had reached the back of the car now. She spun the bike into a full circle and sped back towards the Bouillards. As a band played to signal the last floats passing by on the river, people climbed back into their cars and the traffic began to move again.

"That icing will keep them from following us for a few minutes," yelled Alice. "It should be enough time to lose them."

Eva threw back her head and laughed. The traffic was picking up speed now and Eva had to accelerate to catch up with the Bouillards.

"Where are we heading?" shouted Eva.

"We'll go to Claude's. He'll get them to safety," Alice yelled, and began to shout directions to Eva. As they passed the Bouillards, Eva waved at them to follow her, and they dashed off the bridge and into the city.

Thirty minutes later they were crowded round the kitchen table in Claude's flat. Madame Bouillard was sipping hot coffee while Monsieur Bouillard soothed the children. Albie the cat had, according to Marie, yowled his head off since leaving the house, but after Claude found him a tin of pilchards at the back of a cupboard he had quietened down and was now curled up on Marie's lap. Eva was telling Marie's younger brother all about what it was like to work as a fashion model, demonstrating some of the more ridiculous poses to make him laugh. Claude was tearing a strip off Alice.

"You should have come directly to me instead of dashing off like that," he raged.

"There wasn't time to find you," said Alice. "I couldn't even make it to HQ. I didn't know when the enemy agents would come for them. We got there with minutes to spare."

Claude ran a hand through his hair. "You realise that they might have captured you, and goodness knows how much danger you put Eva in."

Alice's face fell. She felt bad about involving Eva yet again. Hopefully, the spies that were chasing them would not connect the terrifying motorcyclist with the charming young woman who delighted the stages of Paris's fashion houses.

Claude stopped shouting and sighed. "What put you on to them?" he asked.

"Charles Deforges. He has been sewing beads into the frocks to give away addresses in Morse. He made such a fuss about Eva's dress, chopping some of the beads off, and he had just taken a phone call. He must have been given the wrong address and after the phone call he put it right and sent Eva out on to the stage."

"So that's how the addresses have been being passed," said Claude. "It's perfect. Deforges would not need to know who he was passing them to. All he would know was a voice on the phone. No way of making the connection between him and anyone else in the ring."

"What will we do now?" asked Alice.

"We'll take care of him," said Claude. "Give me five minutes to get a message to HQ and they can take him in for questioning. We may still have time to save Léo and Isabella. Well, it looks like I have a few visitors for tonight at least. I'm sorry for snapping, Alice. I just… Well, I do worry about you, you know. You've done well."

Eva crossed the room towards them.

"I've had the most fascinating talk with Madame Bouillard," she said. "She's been telling me all about the new fabrics that are being developed in America. I wish she could meet Monsieur Fouray."

Alice thought for a moment. "Why is Madame Bouillard so important to the enemy?" she asked Claude. "What would they want with her?"

"She is something of a genius in materials science," he said. "Developing stronger fabrics, woven through with metal, that are both light and resilient to damage – even, possibly, to bullets."

"Something that would be useful in planes," Alice said.

Claude nodded. "Very much so. Why?"

"That's the link!" Alice cried. "It must be the link. The Daedalus plot and the fashion hall. That's what draws it all together. You said that Isabella, the agent who's missing, is an expert in our airfields. And Léo – he's an aeronautics engineer. And now we have Madame Bouillard who is so skilled with the very materials that could make a plane safer – or more dangerous to the enemy. Don't you see? They are all people who could help build the most powerful plane and use it against France."

Claude stared at her. "You're right, but—"

Alice cut him off. "And there's another link," she

said. "When I first met Sophie, she was coming from the fashion hall – she'd been sent to get some webbing or something by her father. And later I saw those men, Paul and Victor. They were there too. What if *they* were looking at fabrics for use in planes as well? That could mean that it *is* them who are involved in the Daedalus plot. They keep hanging around Sophie and her father and they've been at the fashion hall too. It *can't* be a coincidence."

"Alice, we've been through this," said Claude. "Sophie's glider is impressive, but it's tiny. There is no way that they would be interested in it. The enemy are looking for the plans for the Daedalus. By all accounts it is one of the most powerful machines ever created. They would be more interested in the fighter planes in the pavilion, not some tiny glider. I told you who our main suspect is, the woman working on the Golden Kite. And she was talking with five people this afternoon who we *know* are friendly with members of the enemy's government. I have two agents in the aviation hall now, keeping a very close eye on her."

"What are you two on about?" asked Eva.

Alice and Claude had not noticed her wander

over. They exchanged a glance.

"I think we can trust her," said Alice. "After all, she's helped us so much tonight, and I'm pretty sure it's Paul and Victor we are after, not anyone from fashion."

Claude hesitated for a few moments and then, in far fewer words than Alice would have used, he let Eva know exactly how much was at stake.

Her face registered utter shock. "Alice," she whispered finally. "Is he telling me you are a spy?"

Alice grimaced. "I thought you might have guessed by now," she said.

Eva shrugged. "Well, when you got us to chase after that woman with the peacock hat, I just thought you were clever and a bit bored."

"And when we rescued the Bouillards?" Alice asked.

"Well, I thought maybe they were hiding from debt collectors. Oh, don't look at me like *that*! How was I meant to know you were a spy? That's the last thing I would have thought of. How much danger have you been putting yourself in all this time?"

"Quite a lot," said Claude. "And no doubt there will be more before we track down the Daedalus plans."

"Daedalus?" asked Eva. "Like in the story of Icarus?"

Alice looked blank.

"You *must* know the story of Icarus," Eva said. "I had to play him last year in some ridiculous show that Charles put together for a collection Monsieur Fouray designed around feathers. Icarus and his father tried to escape from Crete using wings they had made from feathers and wax, but Icarus flew too close to the sun and his wings melted. It's supposed to be a fable about not thinking too much of yourself, but I'm not sure that Charles paid too much attention to that bit."

Something sparked at the back of Alice's mind. What was it that Victor had said to Sophie only the other day? *You could fly to the sun and back.* She had thought at the time that it was a strange thing to say.

"What has that to do with Daedalus though?" she asked Eva.

Eva brushed a stray hair out of her eyes.

"Well, that was Icarus's father. He was called Daedalus."

Alice stared at her.

You could fly to the sun and back.

She turned slowly to Claude.

"Daedalus," she said. "What if Daedalus isn't a set of plans? What if it's a plane, something already made? That's why they've been hanging around with Sophie so much, making notes about her work. They don't want plans, they want the plane."

"Monsieur Alain's plane?" asked Claude. "I've heard he's a skilled aeronautics engineer, but still it's far too small—"

"No, not Monsieur Alain's," said Alice. "Sophie's. They talk with Monsieur Alain, but I've never seen them take the slightest interest in his plane. It's always Sophie's that they want to draw."

"Alice, think straight," said Claude. "From what you've told me, it's little more than a glider. It's no use to the enemy at all. It sounds impressive, I grant you, but the enemy are hardly going to put two agents to work stealing the scribbles of a young girl."

Alice bristled. It was just like when Claude had

said she would only be interested in the fashion hall because she was a "young girl". Claude had the irritating habit of underestimating people because they were younger than him. He did it with Alice and now he was doing the same with Sophie.

"She's a very talented engineer—" she started, but Claude cut her off.

"I don't doubt that for a second, but listen. Why would they steal the plans of one glider? It's not going to get them very far. These people need plane plans, armaments, new guns. They want a whole machinery of war and they need bright brains to create it for them."

Alice's thoughts whirled. Bright brains. Sophie's brain was very bright indeed. "The finest engineer of her generation" – that was what her father had called her. Alice had no doubt that her new friend was capable of all sorts of new inventions.

Alice felt her stomach suddenly turn to ice.

"Claude," she said, trying to keep her voice from shaking. "What if they don't want to steal the plans to Sophie's glider? What if they want to steal *Sophie*?"

The look on Claude's face told her that she could

be right. Alice felt the coldness rush through her. And then she was on fire. Red-hot anger that anyone would try to harm one of her friends. She pushed her chair away from the table.

"Alice, wait," warned Claude, making a grab for her arm.

Alice shook him off and ran for the door. Her hand had almost reached the handle when Eva's closed on it and wrenched the door open.

"You're not going anywhere without me, Alice Éclair," Eva said, and she grabbed the two motorcycle helmets from the table.

Ten minutes later, Alice and Eva rounded the corner by the Palais de l'Air and screeched to a halt. Alice threw herself off the motorbike and pelted through the doors of the pavilion, almost colliding with a small child who was pleading to be allowed to sit in one of the planes. Alice sidestepped them quickly and dashed towards the stairs to the upper level. She must get to Sophie and warn her somehow. She ran across the walkways, Eva close on her heels, and began to climb the stepladder to the roof, hoping that nobody had locked it. At the top she paused, listening for voices, but through the metal door she could hear nothing. She pushed at the trapdoor tentatively and to her relief it gave way. Alice peered out.

Ariadne had been pushed to the edge of the roof, where two blocks of wood sat under her front wheels, holding her in place. A rope tied to her back wing secured her further. Sophie stood with Victor and Paul, examining her left wing.

Alice decided against creeping out. It would look more natural if she pretended that nothing was wrong. Instead, she flung the trapdoor open and clambered out, motioning to Eva to stay back out of sight.

"Alice, you're here!" Sophie cried, dashing across and giving her a quick hug. Alice smiled at her. She noticed a look pass between Victor and Paul.

"I know your father said you were working, but I'll be as quiet as a mouse, I promise," Alice said. "And if you need me to pass you anything—"

"Oh, I'm all finished," said Sophie. "Sorry – I think I got oil on your shoulder."

"That doesn't matter," Alice shrugged, trying to keep her voice light. "Well then, if you're finished, perhaps we could go and find somewhere for a cup of hot chocolate or some lemonade?"

Sophie glanced back at Victor and Paul, who were now deep in conversation. "I promised I would go for one with Victor and Paul," she said. "But we can all go together, if you don't mind lots of boring talk about aeroplanes."

"There's nothing boring about Ariadne!" Alice cried. "And I've brought my friend Eva. She's been dying to meet you." There was absolutely no way that she was going to let Sophie out of her sight for a moment, and certainly not to go anywhere alone with Paul and Victor.

"Alice is coming too!" Sophie called out. "So we'll have to go somewhere that has excellent cake because she has *very* high standards."

"Surely Alice doesn't want to listen to a lot of boring engineering talk," Victor said, wandering over to join them.

"I wouldn't dream of missing out," said Alice.

Victor looked at her very hard. Then he reached out a hand and clasped her collar. Alice drew back, but his grip was firm as he flicked it upright to look at the button pinned to her coat.

"So careless to have it in plain sight," he said. "We've been very patient putting up with your presence, but you *had* to be pushy, didn't you. It looks like our plans really *are* going to change. I was hoping to do this away from the crowds, but you really leave me no choice. The Daedalus plan begins now."

Paul stepped forward, whipped a gun from his pocket and held it against Sophie's temple.

CHAPTER NINETEEN

"No!" cried Alice, hating the look of terror on her friend's face.

Victor held up a warning hand to stop her dashing forwards. He drew a gun from his own pocket and pointed it at Alice.

"It wasn't meant to be like this," he said in a disappointed tone. "We had planned something much more discreet. If only you hadn't interfered, Mam'selle Éclair."

Alice stared at him.

"How do you know my name?" she demanded.

"Oh, we have our sources," Paul said. "Your uncle suggested that you weren't only here to sell cakes."

Alice's heart sank. Of course, they had got information out of Uncle Robert. For a moment, Alice wondered where he was. Then she shook the thought out of her mind. She had to concentrate.

"And when we found out that you were spending quite so much time at the Palais de l'Air..." Paul went on. "Well, it looked suspicious."

"Are... Are you going to shoot me?" asked Sophie, her voice trembling.

Paul looked hurt. "Shoot you? Sophie, you are *very* valuable to us. You are going to be one of our honoured guests. We have some very clever people who are looking forward to talking to you. And we have some new friends for you to meet. You're all coming for an adventure."

"Isabella and Léo!" cried Alice. "Where are you keeping them?"

"Nowhere you need to worry about," Paul snapped.

"All that is going to happen," continued Victor, "is that we are going to leave the building, very quietly and without raising any fuss, and we are going to take you to meet some friends of ours. If either of you causes us any trouble... Well, I don't want to, but if I have to, I will shoot you. Do you understand?"

Sophie gave the tiniest of nods and whimpered.

Victor clicked the catch on the gun and motioned towards the trapdoor. Alice threw Sophie a look that she hoped said "don't worry" and began to edge backwards. She tried desperately to remember whether there was anything she had seen the last time she was on the roof that might help them. She knew that in a moment she would pass Sophie's workbench and tried to recall what was on it. There were tools, heavy ones, but there was no way that she would be able to use any of them to defend herself against Victor's and Paul's guns. In her mind's eye she scanned the rest of the bench. Spanners, a few notes that Sophie had scribbled on paper, a can of oil, a tin of ball bearings. Another image sprang to her mind – Delphine struggling to keep her balance backstage as the pot of silver sugar balls cascaded across the floor.

Alice blinked. As she passed the bench, she stepped sideways so that her hand brushed against the wood. Her palm closed around the tin, and with a sudden movement she swiped it to the floor. The tin burst open, hundreds of tiny beads scattering everywhere. Victor's foot shot forwards from underneath him and he fell headlong to the floor. His gun flew to one side and scuttered into a corner. With a cry, Paul also went down, accidentally flinging his own gun high into the air so that it fell over the side of the parapet. Far below they heard a bang as it went off. Sophie grabbed hold of one of Ariadne's wings and steadied herself.

"Sophie, run," Alice yelled, leaping the steady tide of spreading ball bearings to reach her.

Paul was struggling to his feet. Alice leaned out a hand and pushed him against the workbench. It collapsed under his weight and he sprawled across the floor. Victor was on his feet and, stepping between the ball bearings, made his way towards his gun.

"I'm not leaving them with Ariadne," Sophie said, gripping the plane's wing.

"They don't *care* about Ariadne," Alice cried. "It's you they want." She glanced back at Victor. He had almost reached his gun.

"We won't make it to the trapdoor anyway," Alice shouted. She dragged Sophie away from the wing, grabbed a hammer that was lying on the floor and took a swipe at the blocks of wood under the wheels of the glider. The plane juddered as the wood fell away and began to sway from side to side. Alice hauled herself over the side and into the plane.

"Get in!" she yelled.

"Wait!" Sophie cried, dashing to the front of the plane and spinning the propeller into action. As the plane veered from side to side and pulled against the rope that anchored it to the roof, Sophie jumped into the front seat. Alice was about to shout at her to take them off the roof when, with a sickening drop of her stomach, she realised she had leapt into the pilot's seat.

"Just get us out of here," cried Sophie, reaching over her seat to pull at the rope looped over the back fin. Victor began to turn, the gun in his hand. Sophie grasped the rope and wrenched it over the fin. The plane leapt forwards. Victor pulled the trigger.

And they began to fall.

"Pull the lever in front of you and we'll bank left," Sophie yelled. "We can go down the river and head to the Chaillot."

Alice was barely listening. Her instincts had kicked in and she found she remembered everything that Sophie had told her the night they'd had their short flight over the city. She pulled on the lever that tilted the wing flaps and watched as the needle on the dial showing their angle of flight moved back to steady. She was pulling on the lever to bank them right as they headed over the river when there was an almighty crash behind them and the sound of screaming. She saw Sophie turn and her face registered absolute terror.

"It's Victor and Paul!" she yelled. "They've stolen the Golden Kite!"

Alice allowed herself to glance backwards. There was a gaping hole in the glass side of the Palais de l'Air and the luxurious plane from the middle of the exhibition was quickly gaining on them, trailing its velvet rope. Alice pulled hard on the lever and Ariadne rose further into the sky, but it was no use.

"We can't outrun them!" she cried to Sophie.

There was a pause, during which Alice could only hear the roars of the two planes, then Sophie shouted back, "Are you strapped in?"

"Yes, why?"

"Alice, this is going to be very dangerous, but if we loop then we can avoid them. And they'll not have time to bank and come back towards us."

"Loop?"

"Yes!" Sophie shouted. "I'll talk you through it. Check Ariadne's wing on the left."

"Got it!" shouted Alice, feeling her stomach *already* doing loops.

"Now, keep her pinned to that level while you pull the stick back. She'll start to slow, but keep her steady or we'll drop out of the sky. When we reach the top of the loop, you're going to want to speed her up and control her back down. Now, GO!"

Trying not to think about the words "we'll drop out of the sky", Alice pulled on the controls and the nose of the aeroplane rose in front of her. In moments they were flying vertically and Alice felt the blood in her ears deafening her to everything. As they reached the top of the loop, she began to feel light-headed. Below she could see the Golden Kite with the two men in it fly beneath them, unable to slow its course. Victor's furious face glared up at her from within the cockpit, but with a start, Alice realised that it was not Paul beside him. The terrified face of the flight steward looked up at her.

"Pull her back *now*!" Sophie yelled from the front seat. Alice began to ease off on the stick and the plane dropped sickeningly towards the river below, then curved round into the loop and soon they were level again, flying along the Seine with Victor and Paul in the Golden Kite ahead of them.

"Now bank towards the Chaillot!" Sophie yelled, but Alice shook her head.

"We can't let them get away!" she cried. "They've taken a hostage!"

She willed Ariadne on after the two men, watching as the plane in front tried to bank to turn round and come after them again. If she could force them down safely, she still had time to bring herself and Sophie to rest in the open square near the palace. But how could she do that?

She scanned the surroundings as they flew down the river. The trees on either side glistened with recent rainfall. Something Sophie had said earlier flashed through her mind. A tree covered in spiders' webs. She suddenly had a memory of the dough clogging up the blades of the mixer her mother had bought.

"Sophie! Where is your tree? Is it nearby?"

"What! Why do—"

"Ask me later. Just answer."

"It's on the next bend," Sophie yelled, the confusion evident in her voice. "Keep her steady. Left-hand side of the bank. Take care though; it's a willow and it overhangs the river a lot. You won't see it coming."

"Perfect," yelled Alice. "Hold on!"

She banked Ariadne to the right and pushed down on the throttle to urge her forward. Victor and

Paul were trying to slow down, but she knew that if they slowed too much they could crash. She was gaining on them, pushing the plane to the right so that they would be forced left. They moved further into the bank. Alice held her breath as they rounded the corner, and there it was, just as Sophie had said, a willow tree overhanging the river, its branches a maze of spiders' webs.

And the Golden Kite flew straight into it.

Please work! Alice thought. *Please, please work.* Ahead of her the plane was struggling, the propeller wrapped in long willow fronds and sticky webbing. Alice heard it splutter and die and the plane began to dive. The breath caught in her throat as she thought of how terrified the woman inside must be, and then it pulled level and began to glide, slowly edging towards the water until, with a splash, it ploughed into the river and came to a halt, bobbing unsteadily.

"Now take us down!" Sophie yelled. Alice tipped them sideways and they turned, the plane shuddering from side to side. As they crossed one of the city's bridges into the glare of the sun, the shadow of the plane passed over the crowds below, making them glance upwards. Alice saw a group of children pointing excitedly at them. And then they were heading over the ornamental pool leading to the Chaillot Palace. A crowd pouring out of the Agricultural pavilion pushed forwards to watch as they glided above the carefully trimmed trees and urns bursting with flowers, past the marble statues that lined the pool and towards the theatre in the middle of the curve of the palace.

"Ease off and let her drift down!" Sophie cried. "It's not going to be smooth but with any luck we've got time to not crash."

As they reached the end of the pool Alice felt the wheels of the plane bump against the ground. The wings tilted and the plane began to slow. Alice's teeth gritted as she held the plane steady, and they rattled to a stop in front of the Theatre pavilion and were instantly surrounded by crowds of people chattering and taking photographs.

CHAPTER TWENTY

Alice let out a great sigh of relief. In the front seat, Sophie released herself from her safety belts and turned round, her face full of admiration.

"That was amazing!" she cried.

"We need to get back to the river," said Alice. "Paul and Victor are still free and they have that hostage. We have to rescue her."

Sophie nodded and the two of them scrambled out of their seats and tumbled over the side of the glider, landing in the middle of the gathering crowd. They were instantly surrounded by people asking questions about the glider and demanding to know who they were. Alice tugged at Sophie's elbow and was trying to drag her through the crowd when above the hubbub of the crowd she heard the roar of a motorbike. Speeding down the pavement towards the Chaillot Palace, ignoring the shouts of passers-by, was Eva. Behind her on the pillion seat, Alice caught a glimpse of Claude's worried face.

"It's Eva and Claude," shouted Alice, pulling Sophie along behind her.

The motorbike drew up and Claude leapt off the back and pulled off his helmet.

"Thank goodness you're safe!" Eva cried. "Those

two men were *hopping mad* when you escaped like that. They made a beeline for the exit. I ducked behind a pillar to watch where they went. I was going to follow them, but then they took the Golden Kite so—"

"We haven't got time," Alice said. "We need to get back to the river. Victor and Paul could escape and they have a hostage. We have to save her."

The crowd continued to press on them till Claude turned on them and snapped, "Mam'selle Alain will not be answering any questions today. If you wish to discuss her work with her you must return later this evening when her glider will be *officially* unveiled."

There were mutterings and a couple of brave souls looked as though they were about to try to engage Sophie in further discussion, but there was something about Claude that made people behave as he wanted, and in very little time the crowd began to disperse.

"I think this part should be left to Alice and me," said Claude.

Alice nodded. She looked at Eva.

"We've asked so much of you already, Eva," she said. "But could you help us one last time? Would you be able to hide Sophie somewhere, and her father too?"

Eva nodded. "I know just the place. You'd better get going." She handed Alice a helmet and looked at Claude.

"Ever ridden a motorbike?" she asked.

Claude nodded. "I am trained in all modern vehic—"

"Never mind that, just don't scrape her." Eva grabbed Sophie's hand and they headed back in the direction of the fair.

Alice and Claude watched them leave, then Claude turned to her.

"And now we end this," he said.

"To the left!" yelled Alice as they headed over the bridge. Down in the water she could see Victor and Paul swimming to shore. The woman in the steward's uniform was clinging to the plane, sobbing.

Claude threw the motorbike round the corner and headed for the bank where Victor was dragging himself out. They screeched to a halt and jumped off.

Victor hauled himself upright and started to run,

with Claude following close on his heels. Paul had almost reached the bank. Alice ran towards him, but as she reached him, the woman by the plane went underwater.

Alice froze. Paul was dragging himself out of the water. She could stop him. She could grab his hands and hold him down till Claude got back, but the woman in the water didn't have much time.

Alice's mind raced. If she didn't stop Paul then he would get away, but at what price? Two voices came into her head – Claude telling her "there is nothing as important as a human life" and her mother looking deep into her eyes and telling her *she* was important. She watched Paul clamber to his feet and begin to run, then she made up her mind.

Alice dived into the river.

"I'm proud of you," Claude said later as they watched Victor being led away in handcuffs. The air steward was being tended to in an ambulance and kept having to be stopped from hugging Alice.

"If I'd let her drown I would never have forgiven myself," said Alice.

"I wouldn't have forgiven you either," said Claude.

"We'll get Paul eventually. Victor will talk and he can't hide for long."

"We should go back and find Eva," said Alice. "I hope she found somewhere safe for Sophie and her father."

"Oh, they will be well hidden," said Claude. "She's a smart one is that Eva. And brave too. I wouldn't have left them in her care if I didn't trust her."

CHAPTER TWENTY-ONE

Alice followed Claude into the Fashion pavilion, where the final evening show was in full swing. The concierge at the door nodded towards Alice and raised an eyebrow at her empty hands.

"No creations for us this evening, Mam'selle?" he whispered.

"Monsieur Fouray gave me the evening off," Alice whispered back. "As there are no more *Majesté du Jour* to show, he said I should just enjoy the gowns."

"Well, we have a new photographer in today, Mam'selle," he said. "You might want to stand by him for the best view."

Alice glanced over to the side of the stage where the press usually gathered. Standing there was a man in a brown greatcoat with a wide-brimmed hat pulled rather too low down over his ears. As Alice walked towards him he turned, waved his camera at her and gave her a huge wink. It was Monsieur Alain, but there was no sign of Sophie.

Up on the stage, Monsieur Fouray was introducing the next model. He caught Alice's eye and smiled broadly at her.

"Next up is the delightful Angelique, wearing *Spring Nocturne*," he said. A model that Alice had never seen before walked on to the stage, dressed in a tea gown of baby-blue silk on which hollyhocks and daisies were embroidered. The cape of the gown fluttered at her shoulders and the fluted hem gave her a skipping look as she walked across the stage. Alice tugged at Claude's arm and they seized the opportunity of the audience's attention being elsewhere to slip backstage and find Eva and Sophie.

Eva was standing by the curtain that led to the stage. She had changed out of her day dress into a glittering evening gown covered from head to toe in silver bugle beads. Sophie, however, was not with her, and Alice dashed over and rather too loudly demanded where she was hidden.

"Shh, they'll hear you onstage," said Eva. "Don't worry, she's quite safe. I hid her where absolutely no one would think of looking for her. Now, get out of the way. Angelique is coming offstage."

They stepped back so that they would not be seen as the curtain was drawn back, and the model called Angelique stepped through to be given a quick hug by Delphine, who was about to step out in a chiffon georgette hand-painted evening dress.

"You did brilliantly," whispered Delphine, before slipping past her and out into the spotlight.

"You really did," hissed Eva. She turned to Claude and Alice. "What do you think? Wasn't it a brilliant hiding place? No one would suspect an oil-covered engineer to be one of Monsieur Fouray's glamorous models."

Alice stared at Angelique. Underneath the carefully coiffured hair and the gloss of mascara and lipstick, it was Sophie grinning back at her.

"Well, I *never* would have recognised you!" she cried.

"It's a little different to my usual look, isn't it," giggled Sophie. "And it was enormous fun. Monsieur Fouray was such a pet to let me take part." For a moment her face clouded over. "But what happened with Paul and Victor?"

Claude patted her on the shoulder. "No need to worry about them," he said. "We have Victor and soon we'll get Paul too, thanks to you two."

Sophie laughed. Then she suddenly sprang forward and hugged first Eva and then Claude and Alice.

"Now then," Claude said. "No crying. You've

got to have clear vision if you're going to fly that plane tonight. Which reminds me – first we need to organise someone to winch it back up to the top of the Palais de l'Air. You three stay here and enjoy the rest of the show while I see to that."

Whisking something away from under his eye, the older spy set off, leaving Alice, Sophie and Eva to applaud Delphine as she came back from her tour of the room.

The grand finale of the World Fair was a blaze of colour and light. The Chaillot Palace was abuzz with visitors and with circus performers weaving their way through the crowds on stilts or with flaming juggling balls. Alice was seated at a table outside the palace with Monsieur Alain, raspberry cordials and black cherry sorbets topped with sparklers, waiting for Sophie to make her grand entrance in her plane. Claude had been as good as his word and a collection of agents from HQ had made sure that Ariadne was transported back to the Palais de l'Air and winched up on to the roof where Sophie could check that her earlier flight had not damaged her in any way. Monsieur Alain had insisted on buying

Alice every cordial and dessert on the menu, and she was surrounded by more raspberry fizzes, black cherry sorbets and chocolate cakes than she could hope to get through in one evening. Alice was just telling him again that he really didn't have to buy her anything else when they were joined by Claude and Eva.

"There you are!" cried Eva, weaving her way past a woman in a sequined costume on the top of a unicycle. She threw herself into a chair and dropped a large ribboned box on to the chair beside Alice.

"I bring news and Eva brings gifts," Claude said, drawing a chair to the table and looking with vague amusement at the cluster of glasses and dessert bowls in front of Alice.

"News?" said Alice.

"*Good* news. Victor has confessed to where Isabella and Léo are. Our operatives rescued them an hour ago and they are safe. And it's all down to you, Alice."

"And Eva," said Alice.

Eva waved the praise aside and nudged the box towards Alice.

"Come on and open it. I'm desperate to know

which one he picked. He wouldn't let me help at all."

"He?" asked Alice.

"Monsieur Fouray. He said it was a thank-you present for everything you did to stop that awful Monsieur Lenoir stealing his designs. He's in a good mood this evening because he's scored something of a coup. Elisabet Aubert has ordered six of his gowns. Señor Rubio is *furious*. Apparently he tried to create something with moving parts for her, like your amazing cake. He thought it would be *ever* so modern and daring, but all it did was catch her hair. She's lost a great clump from the back of her scalp and she is furious with him. Serves him right for trying to steal an idea from you, the big faker."

Alice grinned and leaned forwards to untie the ribbons, but as she did so, a great gasp rose up from the crowd. She looked out and saw that they were pointing into the air.

"Here," said Claude, handing her a pair of binoculars. Alice looked up into the night sky. Across the horizon came first one and then another glowing light as the hot-air balloon display headed towards the city. Within minutes the sky above them was full of glowing balloons, their colours flaming brightly, lit by the fire of the braziers in the baskets slung underneath. Alice scoured the sky to see whether Sophie had managed to join them, but she couldn't see her. She focused on the roof of the Palais de l'Air and saw a stream of lights launch itself into mid-air.

"There she is!" Alice cried. "She has strung Ariadne with fairy lights so we can see her!"

They watched as the brightly lit plane grew closer and closer, weaving between the balloons that floated overhead. Then, as she neared the Chaillot Palace, Sophie executed a perfect loop-the-loop, the lights on her plane dancing in the air to loud exclamations from the crowd.

"She's coming in to land!" Eva cried as Sophie began to descend, gliding effortlessly over the pool in the middle of the square, almost clipping the statues that surrounded it, and swooping to a halt among the lanterns at the end nearest the palace itself. The crowd exploded into applause and Sophie stood up in Ariadne, triumphant and smiling.

It was quite some minutes before Sophie was

able to make her way through the gathered crowd wanting to congratulate her, and the newspapers and photographers wanting a story about France's greatest new young engineer, but eventually Sophie made it to their table and dropped into the chair that Claude had commandeered for her.

"You'll never guess who helped me launch from the roof," she said. "Monsieur Fouray! He wants to plan an entire winter range around aeroplanes. He says I've inspired him! Oh, and he's bringing me that lovely gown he let me wear. I want to change into it for the parties after midnight, because I don't think I'll ever be at anything quite as exciting as this again."

"Don't you believe it," said Alice. "You're going to be a famous aviator. You were amazing."

"You're all amazing," said Claude. "I'm proud to know each and every one of you." He turned to Alice. Now, talking of gowns, and honestly I have had enough talk of them for a lifetime, I think that Alice was about to open a gift herself.

Alice laughed and pulled open the bow on the top of the box. The ribbons fell away and she lifted the lid to reveal layers of peach tissue paper. She peeled them back and pulled out a froth of organza, cream melting into peaches and pinks and finishing in a cascade of blue. She gasped.

"*Joie du Printemps*," she said. "But this must be worth a fortune."

"Quite a bit, but then so are Monsieur Fouray's design secrets," said Eva. "He said he may never be able to thank you enough, but he hopes this goes some way. And you will always be welcome at a Monsieur Fouray show. And he said … oh I hope he turns up soon and he can tell you himself. I hate playing messenger."

Alice held the gown against herself, taking care to keep it safely away from the melting red of the sorbets. "It's the most beautiful thing I've ever owned," she said. "And it looks like it will be a perfect fit."

"That will be the skill of a good designer," said Claude. "A really exceptional one can make clothes fit to perfection just by looking at a person."

Alice glanced at Claude and grinned.

"So next time we have a mission, can *I* be the glamorous one?" she asked.

Claude laughed. Alice started to pack the dress

away into the box, but Sophie stopped her. "Oh, don't put it away. Wait till Monsieur Fouray arrives with my dress and we'll go and change and join the dancing," she said.

Alice grinned and looked around the table at her friends. Whatever her next mission brought, whether she was dressed as a glamorous aristocrat or, as usual, one of the staff, she knew that she would be glad. She would be serving France and helping people while working alongside the bravest spies in the world.

But tonight she would dance in the middle of the Chaillot Palace with a model who rode motorbikes like the wind and the world's most talented young engineer while the sky exploded with light above them. Because tonight she was not France's youngest spy. She was simply Alice Éclair, happy and among friends at the most glamorous party the city had ever seen.

Acknowledgements

The idea for this book came when I was reading about events in Paris in the 1930s. A grand exhibition was held in the city over six months in 1937. The whole world really did come to Paris and great pavilions for each nation were built, as well as specialist halls for arts, crafts, industry and technology. At the same time, the nations were preparing for possible war and their pavilions were used as demonstrations of their might. The World Fair that Alice attends is a fictionalised version of the exposition. There must have been so much espionage going on behind the scenes so it felt like the ideal setting for her next spy adventure.

I have so many people to thank for bringing this book to life. Thank you to Joanna Moult, my incredible agent, for always championing Alice, and for phone calls that make me laugh and stop me panicking. Massive thanks to Fiona Scoble, whose editing is always as kind and encouraging as it is accurate and wise. Thank you for always challenging me to make things better and for believing that I can.

Thank you to everyone at Nosy Crow, especially Nic Theobold and Elisabetta Barbazza for their amazing design work on Alice's covers, Jono Ganz for the animations that made me squeal with delight, Hannah Prutton for being Alice's most incredible cheerleader in all things marketing and the awesome rights team for making sure Alice has a passport to travel the world. Huge thanks to Beatriz Castro for illustrations that make me want to dash back to Paris instantly and watch fireworks over the Eiffel Tower.

Family and friends, as ever, have been supremely supportive, few more so than Debbie Moon, who is always a cheerful text away with wise writing advice. Debs, this one is for you, in recognition of the exhibitions and galleries we have walked together.

And to you, my lovely readers, thank you so much. I'm really grateful to all the readers, teachers, librarians and booksellers who have supported Alice's adventures. I've loved meeting you and talking to you, and I hope to meet more of you now that her second mission is out in the world.

As always, to my husband, Neil, you are a rock and I truly appreciate how much you care about me being happy writing over having a tidy house or an ordered life. I love you lots. xxx